SHADOW GUARDIAN

AND THE BOYS THAT WENT WOOF

Shadow Guardian Series

Shadow Guardian

and the Boys That Went Woof

Robert J. Lewis

4 Horsemen
Publications, Inc.

As always, this is dedicated to my beloved parents, Robert O. Lewis and Dolores C. Lewis. I know they are smiling down at me as proud as can be. To my darling diva Bonita who has been a welcome distraction and cuddle buddy when I needed her. To my Bonita Boys, William, Randy, Chris, Brian, Kalvin, Rodney, Jeff, and Berto. Without your support, I don't know where I would be.

I'd also like to give a special dedication to two individuals who may not realize they contributed a great deal to this book, Pup TyDa and Pup Victor. You're good boys.

In this book I have Pups. I had to learn a lot about Pup culture to properly represent them in this book. I spoke with and messaged actual Pups to make sure I have customs right and terminology correct. My journey into the Pup world has shown me how truly special, wonderful, and spectacular all of you are. Thank you for allowing me into it. I would especially like to thank Pup TyDa and Pup Victor. You're good boys.

TABLE OF CONTENTS

CHAPTER 1

S HADOW GUARDIAN CROUCHED ON the rooftop. Below, the blaring alarm of the jewelry store echoed through the streets, ignored. Shadow Guardian gritted his teeth. With the mayoral and police chief elections looming on the horizon, Mayor Trainer and his lackey, Police Chief Brutus, were still ignoring the Northside's problems.

"Shadow Voice to Shadow Guardian," Alex's voice brought Shadow Guardian out of his thoughts. "I've got three armed robbers, and it looks like..." Alex paused, "...they are wearing pig masks."

Standing, Shadow Guardian spat out the words. "The Three Little Pigs."

"This is their fifth robbery this week," Alex commented. "They're coming out."

Shadow Guardian took a few steps back. "Time to make these little piggies go wee-wee-wee all the way to jail."

Running toward the side of the building, Shadow Guardian leaped up over the edge. Curling into a ball, he spun twice before uncurling and sending two Shadow tendrils out to attach to the surrounding buildings to slow his fall. When he was five feet from the ground, he withdrew them and landed on his feet ten feet from the jewelry store entrance.

Three portly men in pig masks carrying bags over their shoulders and brandishing guns came rushing out. Upon seeing Shadow Guardian standing there, the lead piggy suddenly stopped, causing the two behind him to collide with him. The Piggies took a step back when they saw the shadowy figure blocking their escape.

"This is our score, freak," the lead piggy said, raising his gun. "Go find your own."

The piggy to the right spoke up, "Brick, that's Shadow Guardian."

"I don't care who he is, Straw, he isn't getting our score," Brick sniped back.

The other piggy chimed in. "I'm Straw. He's Sticks."

"Not now!" yelled Brick, keeping his gun aimed at Shadow Guardian. "Shoot this bastard!"

With enhanced movements from his suit, Shadow Guardian flung six Shadow Stars. The first three knocked the weapons from their hands, the next three hit their chests and delivered a mild electric shock. The Piggies convulsed momentarily and dropped their ill-gotten loot, spilling it to the ground.

"Surrender," Shadow Guardian commanded.

Brushing off the electrical charge, Brick sneered, "There's still three of us and only one of you."

"Who said I was alone?" Shadow Guardian asked. An ear-piercing howl came from the darkness of the side alley. "Let me introduce you to my little friend."

Yellow eyes pierced through the darkness. A low, rumbly growl came as a paw stepped into the light. "Little pig, little pig," Lobo snarled, stepping into the light.

"What the Hell is that?" Straw asked, panicked.

Shoving Straw and Sticks aside, Brick yelled, "I'm not sticking around to find out!"

The three fell over each other as they tried to run away, only to be thwarted when the bolas shot from the Shadow Drone wrapped around them. Terrified, they struggled in vain against the nylon Kevlar fibers to get away. Three Shadow darts loaded with tranquilizers then lodged into each of them, and the frightened pigs went limp.

"Three piggies all wrapped up and ready to go to market," Alex announced proudly. An arrow with a flash drive containing video of the Three Pigs robbing the store shot into the ground. "You guys better get out of sight. Aaron and his men are ten minutes out."

Lobo jumped into the air and dug his claws into the side of the building. "Meet you at the top."

"A little help Shadow Voice?" Shadow Guardian asked. The Shadow Drone maneuvered to hover over him. Shadow Guardian grabbed the two handholds.

Lifting Shadow Guardian into the air, Alex asked, "Do you want me to send the Shadow Car to come pick you up?"

"Let me check." Shadow Guardian dropped to the rooftop. He looked at Lobo, who was shaking his head. "I think we're going to do it the old-fashioned way."

Lobo bared his teeth in the approximation of a smile. "First one back gets the last piece of Esmerelda's flan."

"Whoops," Alex said over the comms.

Lobo snatched the Shadow Drone out of the air. He snarled into the camera. "What do you mean, whoops?"

"I wanted a snack," Alex answered guiltily.

Shadow Guardian snatched the drone from Lobo. "Tell me you didn't."

"I didn't," Alex lied guiltily. "But I did."

Lobo snarled, "He must be punished."

"Agreed." Shadow Guardian let go of the drone. Turning to Lobo, he said, "Let's go. There's one more villain we need to punish tonight."

Juan Carlos's rooftop garden was peacefully quiet. Hurling himself over the edge, Lobo landed in a crouch on one of the carefully designed pathways. He inhaled deeply, enjoying the sweet smell of the night blooms. Shadow Guardian came gliding down to land beside him. Shadow Guardian's mask retracted, revealing Diego's face.

Lobo chuffed. Red sparkling lights popped around him. His fur rescinded into his skin. Lobo's body began dissolving away while Freddy's body slowly faded in. There was a brief flash of red light leaving Freddy standing in the garden wearing a golden medallion around his neck and a pair of black boxer briefs.

"Transforming is so much easier thanks to this Atlantean medallion." Freddy rubbed the golden disk between his thumb and forefinger.

"These microbot briefs you gave me also help keep my modesty."

Diego clasped Freddy on the shoulder. "It's good to have you back, even if it's for a short time."

"You guys aren't really mad at me, are you?" Alex asked through the hovering drone.

Freddy grinned at Diego. "Let's get him."

"We'll take the garden entrance." Diego tapped a spot on his arm. One of the large paving stones in front of them slid away. "Follow me."

Freddy followed Diego into the passage. Landing beside Diego, he growled, "Where is he?"

"He's hiding." Diego scanned the empty lab. "Come out, Alex! We're not going to hurt you!"

Two Shadow Drones came flying at Diego and Freddy, pelting them with the foam training balls. Alex laughed through the speakers, "Surrender!"

"That asshole!" Freddy laughed, scooping up foam balls and tossing them back at the drones.

Diego ducked and dodged the objects flying at his head. "You know I don't like balls flying at my face!"

"There goes your sex life," Freddy commented with a grin.

Scooping up foam balls from the floor, Diego started pelting Freddy.

"Jerk!" he laughed.

"Hey! I thought we were after Alex!" Freddy started throwing balls at Diego. "He's the one that finished off the flan!"

Diego whipped around and shot out a Shadow Tendril from his outstretched arm. "That's right!" The tendril snaked around the lab to the other side of the desk and wrapped around Alex's ankle. "Got you!"

Alex let out a yelp. "What the Hell?" He was pulled from behind the desk. Sliding across the floor, he bellowed, "No fair! That's cheating!" The tendril released him. Looking up at Diego, he said, "Hi."

"You ate the last of the flan," Freddy growled, moving to stand over Alex with his arms crossed over his bare chest.

Diego reached down and pulled Alex to his feet. "What do you have to say for yourself?"

"That it was delicious," Alex said with a grin.

Diego shook his head. "You better be glad you're cute. We can't get another flan until Esmerelda and Gato get back from Spain."

"What are we going to do to him?" Freddy asked.

"Not we. Me." Diego kissed Alex. "I don't think it's appropriate to tell you."

"You two are almost as bad as me and Salvador." Freddy laughed, shaking his head.

Alex leaned against Diego. "How much longer do you guys have to be there? It's been six months."

"Hopefully not too much longer." Freddy shrugged. "His abilities are odd. He's a siren, but not a siren."

Confused, Alex asked, "What do you mean?"

"Sirens control people with their song, but he," Freddy shook his head, "he can do more. I watched him sing an entire garden to bloom. He manifests things like Esmerelda can with a note. Even the mystics from Avalon can't explain it."

Needing to comfort his brother, Diego reassured him, "Esmerelda will find the answers in Spain. I know it."

"You're right. She will," Freddy said, not believing the words. "I should get going or I'll miss my portal back to Atlantis."

Alex hugged Freddy. "Let us know if you need anything."

"We're here for you," Diego said, joining the hug. He pulled away suddenly. "I almost forgot! I have something for Salvador!"

Looking on curiously, Alex and Freddy watched Diego go to the wall and tap a few buttons. A panel opened. Diego pulled out a small metallic sphere. He tossed it to Freddy. "Here."

"I keep telling you that we don't play fetch," Freddy said, catching it.

Diego rolled his eyes. "It's a blank microbot suit. He can program it with this." Diego pulled out a controller from the wall and tossed it to Freddy.

"He's not going to be a hero," Freddy argued.

Alex shrugged. "Juan Carlos uses his for Drag. Salvador can use his for his concerts."

"Thanks." Freddy pressed the items to his boxer briefs, letting the microbots surround them. "Stay out of trouble."

Red magic popped around Freddy. Fur sprouted out of his skin. Freddy faded away as Lobo transposed on top of him. A brief flash of red light and Lobo stood before Alex and Diego. "You guys know how to reach me if you need me." Lobo leaped up through the hole in the ceiling.

"They totally play fetch." Alex laughed, taking Diego into his arms.

Diego snickered. "Yes, they totally do." He held Alex tight. "Now it's time for your punishment."

"I'm looking forward to it." Alex grinned.

CHAPTER 2

MAYOR TRAINER SAT AT HIS DESK in his home office, staring out the window into the city night. He did not turn around when he heard Chief Brutus slink into the room. He already knew what Brutus was going to tell him. As punishment for his failure, he let the man stand there uneasily, waiting to be acknowledged.

Without turning around, Mayor Trainer said bitterly, "The Three Pigs were arrested by Aaron Heath and his little group of rogue officers."

"Yes, sir," Chief Brutus confirmed, his deep voice full of shame. "They're being booked as we speak."

Mayor Trainer cracked his neck. "We need to silence them before they squeal about our connections with them."

"The news media has already gotten wind of their arrest." Chief Brutus shifted uncomfortably. "They are swarming the police station."

Mayor Trainer slammed his hand down on the armrest. "Go get changed. Now!"

"Yes, sir. I'm sorry, sir." Chief Brutus left with his head hanging down.

Mayor Trainer turned his chair around. He tapped a button on his desk. Two monitors rose from the desk to flank his main screen. He clicked on the meeting icon on his desktop. The new screens came to life, waiting for the others to join. The young demon twink, Dante, appeared first on the left. On the right, the silhouette of a man appeared.

"Gentlemen," Mayor Trainer greeted them. "We have a problem."

Dante steepled his fingers in front of him. "We or you?"

"You're down in the polls," came the modulated voice from the other screen. "You promised us you had this election. Control of Morgan City is key if we are to take over DJC."

Mayor Trainer stifled his anger. "With the device you sent me, I should be able to secure the election."

"That device was not designed for large-scale use," the modulated voice reprimanded. "It doesn't have the power to work on more than a few individuals at a time."

Mayor Trainer gave them a sinister smile. "My associate has been able to ramp up the power."

"And the results?" Dante asked, leaning in with mischievous curiosity.

Mayor Trainer lied smoothly, "Positive."

"I find that hard to believe," the modulated voice scoffed. "If you have all this under control, why contact us? What do you need?"

Mayor Trainer carefully kept the anger of the failure out of his voice. "The Three Pigs were arrested tonight by Aaron Heath and his rogue band of officers. I would take care of them through normal means, but the media has gotten a hold of it."

"That sounds like a 'you' problem and not like an 'us' problem," Dante chided.

Mayor Trainer sneered. "I could make it a 'you' problem, if you like."

"Enough," the modulated voice ordered. "We shall take your Piggies to slaughter, but remember this, Doug Trainer," the modulated voice grew threatening, "we've invested a lot of time and resources into you. We expect a return on our investment soon. Are we understood?"

Swallowing his pride, Mayor Trainer answered, "Understood."

"Good, now I'm sending you video footage of the vigilantes that thwarted the Pigs," the modulated voice said.

Dante hissed, "It was the same group that raided the condo tower and freed the fairy."

"What did I tell you about using slurs like that?" Mayor Trainer snapped.

Dante narrowed his eyes. "It was an actual fairy, you dumbass. Wings and all."

"I stand corrected," Mayor Trainer acquiesced. "I will put the video to good use."

Dante ran a hand down the fluted bottle beside him. "You better. There's enough room in here for you as well."

The screens went blank. Mayor Trainer tapped the button, lowering the screens. Chief Brutus appeared in the doorway. Gone was his police uniform, replaced with shiny black combat boots, tiny shiny red shorts, a bulldog harness, and a leather Doberman puppy mask. He looked as timid as he was threatening.

"Come here, Pup," Mayor Trainer ordered. He admired Pup Brutus's corded muscles as he moved. Stopping at Mayor Trainer's side, he dropped to his knees. Mayor Trainer rubbed the back of Pup Brutus's head. "I know you did your best, boy. You're a good Pup."

Pup Brutus looked up at Mayor Trainer with mournful eyes. "I will not fail you again, sir."

"I know you won't." Mayor Trainer smiled at him. "We'll take this city one way or another. Aaron Heath has rogue do-gooder officers, but we have our Pup Patrol, don't we?"

With a glint in his eyes, Pup Brutus said, "Yes, sir. We have twenty handpicked officers that have gone through the training."

"Good." He patted Pup Brutus on the head. "Have them venture out into the city and find us more suitable Pups for our kennel."

Pup Brutus nodded his head. "Yes, sir."

"Whether I win the election or not, this city will heel at my feet." Mayor Trainer ran a hand over Pup Brutus's hood. Stopping under his chin, Mayor Trainer lifted his head. "Go get our bed ready for bed. I'll be there as soon as I review this video."

Pup Brutus's body shook with excitement. "Yes, sir."

"Let's see who has been helping out our honorable detective and his crew." Mayor Trainer turned back to the screen and opened the file. There was no sound. He watched a shadow of a man lower himself to the ground, then a huge wolf step forth from the alley, and finally a robotic drone zipped around and tied up the pigs before shooting them with a dart. "Vigilantes and monsters."

An arrow with a flash drive shot into the ground, then the trio left, heading up the side of the building. "I'm going to need something special to deal with these meddlers." The video ended. Mayor Trainer opened up a new video call window. After a moment, the screen came to life with a young man with multicolor hair. "Gaymer. I have a job for you."

"Dude, I was in the middle of a game. Now my guy is dead and my squad is all yelling at me." Gaymer slammed back into the chair. "What do you want?"

Mayor Trainer forwarded the video. "I've just sent you a video of some individuals we need to be able to neutralize."

"Fine, whatever." Gaymer leaned forward and opened the email. His eyes went wide when he saw the video. "You're kidding, right? Do you know who that is?"

Mayor Trainer casually said, "Enlighten me."

"That's Shadow Guardian. Word on the net is that he's the one that took down those Three Bear dudes, not to mention all the criminals he's caught over the past few months," Gaymer said in awe. "His tech is awesome. I wish I could get just a peek at it."

Mayor Trainer looked at Gaymer intently through the screen. "Make it happen and make sure the modifications to that device I gave you work. I want this entire city under my control."

"You're asking a lot of me in a short time, man," Gaymer complained.

Mayor Trainer's tone grew stern. "Remember who funds your little ass."

"Whatever," Gaymer said with a huff.

Mayor Trainer wanted to reach through and throttle the young man. Through clenched teeth, he snapped, "You test my patience."

"Are you done? You're interrupting my game time." Gaymer smiled wickedly. "Shouldn't you be having your own playtime with your pooch?"

Mayor Trainer glared at the screen. "His name is Pup Brutus. Show him some respect or I'll let him turn you into his new chew toy."

"Oh, I'm scared," Gaymer mocked. "I identified your man. Is there anything else because I have another campaign to do here in a bit?"

Mayor Trainer's nostrils flared. "Send the videos to all the news outlets anonymously. I don't want it traced back to us. I want it done now."

"I'll get to it," Gaymer griped.

Mayor Trainer's face flushed red with anger. "I want it done now, or do I need to send Pup Brutus to watch over you?"

"I don't have any puppy treats," Gaymer mocked. He tapped a few keys. "Done. Later!"

The video went dead. Mayor Trainer shook his head. "Family."

CHAPTER 3

DIEGO BURST THROUGH THE STAIR entrance. "Open the door! Open the door!" he shouted at the slender blond-haired man with blue frosted tips sitting at the desk in front of Dion's office. "Hurry!"

"We have a code, Diego," Aspen said into the intercom before standing and opening the door to Dion's office.

The elevator door opened behind Diego. A middle-aged woman wearing only her black bra and panties came screeching out after Diego. "I can change you! Just give me a chance!"

"Shut the door! Shut the door!" Diego yelled, running past Aspen. The door slammed shut behind him. Diego slowed to a stop in front of Dion's desk. Trying to catch his breath, Diego said, "I need a new personal assistant."

Dion gave him an unamused look. "I know." She turned up the volume on the intercom.

"Honey, what are you doing?" Aspen's voice came over the speaker. "He's gay, and he has a boyfriend. You're not changing him. Security has been notified. Oh, good. They are here. They'll take you to get your things and escort you out of the building. You'll be paid for the full week. Ta ta."

Dion turned the intercom off. "This makes what? Twenty? Thirty personal assistants?"

"Fifty-seven." Diego collapsed into a chair. "Gay. Straight. Bi. Male. Female. Intersex. They all have been coming after me since they ran that puff piece about me being the most eligible bachelor."

Dion shook her head. "We can't keep going on like this. It's starting to impede our work."

"*We* can't go on like this? I can't go on like this," Diego said, exasperated. "Why can't I use Aspen?"

Dion looked at Aspen, who stepped into the office. "Let's ask him," Dion smirked. "Aspen, why can't you pull double duty as mine and Diego's personal assistant?"

"I prefer not to answer, as it may hurt his feelings," Aspen answered smoothly.

Turning around to look at Aspen, Diego asked, "Why would it hurt my feelings?"

"It just would." Aspen smiled icily at him before sitting in the other chair. "I take it we need to find our company sex symbol another personal assistant?"

Diego snapped, "No!"

"Yes," Dion corrected him. "Aspen, we need to put an end to these Code Diego's."

Puzzled, Diego asked, "Code Diego's?

"We just had one," Aspen clarified.

Diego nodded. "Aww, smart. Now, why won't you be my personal assistant?"

"Diego! Focus!" Dion shouted in frustration.

Guiltily, Diego said, "Sorry."

"This is why you need a personal assistant. The problem is finding one that won't chase you around in their underwear."

Diego snapped his fingers. "I got it! How about—"

"No." Aspen cut him off.

Diego gave him an incredulous look. "You didn't let me finish."

"Whatever it was, it was going to be wrong," Aspen answered.

Dion asked smugly, "Was he wrong?"

"No," Diego sulked.

Leaning back in her chair, Dion asked, "Okay, gentlemen, how are we going to realistically solve this problem?"

"We could get Juan Carlos to vet them," Diego suggested. "Mamacita always looks out for her baby boy."

Aspen pulled out his phone and pulled up a calendar. "That would work if Juan Carlos wasn't booked up doing charity events and campaigning for Detective Aaron Heath and Felipe Montoya. Right now he's checking up on Joshua Waters."

"Right." Diego turned to look at Aspen. "Wait, how do you know his schedule?"

Aspen sat his phone face down on his leg. "I've had to make some travel arrangements for him and assist him with organizing some events."

"Wait. You'll be her personal assistant." Diego pointed at Dion. "You'll be Juan Carlos's personal assistant?" Diego pointed at the phone, then at himself. "But not mine?"

Without even looking at Diego, Aspen said frostily, "Exactly."

"Boys, we need a solution," Dion reprimanded. "How are we going to solve the Diego problem before we get slapped with a sexual harassment suit?"

Sulking, Diego grumbled, "I am not a problem."

"You are the problem," Aspen said frostily. Seeing Dion's glare, he added, "Apologies." Reluctantly, he added, "I may have a solution."

Relieved, Dion said, "Great. Who is it?"

"If Diego can't have me, he can have the next best thing. My brother," Aspen answered, hesitantly. "My twin brother, Aiden. He just came back to town and is looking for work."

Dion cautiously asked, "Are you sure we're not going to have a Code Diego with him?"

"You make it sound like it's my fault. Can we call it something else?" Diego asked. "I did make that paper print a retraction."

Ignoring Diego's comments, Aspen said, "I'm certain of it. Diego is definitely not his type."

"Great, first you won't be my personal assistant and now you're telling me I'm not your brother's type. This conversation is a real ego boost," Diego grumbled.

With a cold smile, Aspen said, "Sorry, he's not into Daddies."

"I am not a daddy!" Diego shot a look at Dion, who was covering her smile with her hand. "I am not a daddy!"

Dion bit back her laughter. "I am so telling Juan Carlos about this."

"I'll have him come in for an interview." Aspen took a deep breath. "I have to warn you, he is a bit fiery."

Dion's smile faded. "What do you mean, fiery?"

"Passionate. Flamboyant. Wild," Aspen clarified. He shook his head. "He'll keep Diego on task and probably encourage him to go off task."

Diego nodded. "Sounds good to me. Bring him in."

"Great. I guess we'll be looking for a bigger apartment." Aspen started typing on his phone. "I'll see if he can come in today."

Diego's phone started ringing. "It's Juan Carlos, hold on." Putting the phone to his ear, he said, "Hey, Mamacita." Diego looked at Aspen and smiled. "I think I have the solution. Hold on." Diego put his hand over the phone. "Aspen, how would you like a three-bedroom apartment rent-free at DJC Tower?"

"A free three-bedroom apartment?" Aspen asked suspiciously. "What's the catch?"

Diego grinned. "You'll be rooming with Joshua Waters and keeping an eye on him for Juan Carlos."

"I want a balcony," Aspen demanded. "And you can't randomly show up and want to hang out."

Diego took his hand away from the phone. "Done. Aspen and his twin brother..." Diego looked at Aspen.

"Aiden," Aspen grunted.

Diego smiled. "Aiden. He's going to be my new personal assistant." Diego rolled his eyes. "Yes, there was another Code Diego. I'll tell you later. Go ahead and get Joshua moved into the apartment. Hasta después."

"Aiden will be here in an hour for an interview. I'll bring him to your office as soon as he gets here." Aspen stood up. "Unless you need me for anything else, I have work to do."

Dion nodded. "Go on, and thank you."

"Diego." Aspen tilted his head to him, then left.

When Aspen shut the door, Diego asked, "Why doesn't he like me?"

"He does. He admires you." Dion leaned forward in her chair. "He told me so in his interview. I think you're just too much for him."

Diego asked, "Too much?"

"He's organized, structured," Dion explained. "You're... you're..."

Diego finished, "Passionate? Flamboyant? Wild?"

"Exactly," Dion answered.

CHAPTER 4

P OUNDING ON THE APARTMENT door, Juan Carlos shouted, "Joshua! Open up! I know you're in there!" He waited a moment before adding, "I'm not going anywhere!"

"Go away!" came the angry shout from the other side.

Refusing to be deterred, Juan Carlos checked to make sure no one else was around before pulling out the small black disc and sticking it to the doorknob. "You're leaving me no choice!" He pulled out his phone and opened the app Alex created to control the microbots. Instructing them to open the door, Juan Carlos said, "Get to work my pretties."

The disc came to life. Juan Carlos watched the microbots disappear into the keyhole. There was an audible click. The microbots poured out and traveled in a straight line up to the deadbolt to repeat the process. He expected them to return to their disc configuration, but instead, they slipped around the edge of the door. Juan Carlos heard the flip of the metal privacy lock. The microbots made their way back around the door and formed a small disc on the door.

"You are amazing." The microbots made a smiling face. "What the?" The smiling face disappeared when Juan Carlos plucked the disc from the door. *I need to tell Alex and Diego about this.*

Putting the disc carefully back in his pocket, Juan Carlos opened the door. His nose wrinkled at the smell. "Aye, dios mio." Juan Carlos took a step into the dark apartment. "Joshua?"

"I said go away!" Joshua shouted from the darkness.

Finding a light switch, Juan Carlos flipped it on. He gasped at the horrible state the apartment was in. Half-empty food containers littered every surface. Flies buzzed around and cockroaches scurried about. Clothes were tossed haphazardly everywhere. A wall sconce hung precariously from its wires.

"Go away!" Joshua shouted from his hiding place. "I don't want to see anyone! I don't want to see you!"

Juan Carlos noticed the mound of clothes on the broken couch moving. Carefully navigating his path there, he said, "Too bad. The agreement to keep you on DJC payroll after the kidnapping requires that we meet once a month." Juan Carlos cringed when he stepped on something squishy, then heard a crunch. "You've been avoiding me for months."

The pile of clothes shifted. "Where have you been, Joshua?" Juan Carlos asked softly. "Your landlord says you disappear for weeks at a time." Moving closer, Juan Carlos added, "She says you look more like a beast than a man." Juan Carlos pushed aside a small pile of trash so he could step around the dilapidated couch. "She's not renewing your lease."

Juan Carlos debated about sitting but ultimately chose not to when he didn't see anything remotely clean. "Joshua, will you, please, come out and talk to me?"

"No," Joshua grunted from under a pile of clothes.

Juan Carlos picked up a piece from the pile with two fingers. "Joshua, please, let me help you."

"I don't need your help," Joshua growled bitterly, sitting up and sending clothes tumbling around him.

Juan Carlos was taken aback by Joshua's appearance. He wore a scraggly, sandy-blond beard. His curly locks were tangled and long in places while cut short in others. What was most disturbing was that Joshua's once cherub face was angular and gaunt and his eyes looked full of anguish and despair.

Reaching out to touch his face, Juan Carlos asked, "Niño, what has happened to you?"

"Nothing." Joshua jerked his face away.

Pulling his hand back, Juan Carlos said, "Something happened. You don't have to talk to me about it now, but you can when you're ready."

"Now that you've seen me, can you go?" Joshua glared at Juan Carlos.

Juan Carlos's slap across his face caught Joshua off guard. "You will not talk to me like that. Do you understand me, chico?" Joshua held a hand to his face. "I tried being nice, now you're getting Mamacita Juan Carlos."

"What does that mean?" Joshua asked, his voice tinged with fear.

Crossing his arms, Juan Carlos said, "What that means is I'm going to talk. You're going to listen and what I tell you to do, you're going to do."

"You're not my dad." Joshua's voice cracked when he spoke.

Juan Carlos made a conceding face. "True, I'm not your mamacita either, but I'm the one here. I spoke with your parents, and they are worried. They haven't heard from you in months."

"I've been busy." Joshua looked down at his feet in shame.

Juan Carlos lifted Joshua's head back up to look at him. "We're going to get you cleaned up." He looked around the apartment. "I guess we set fire to this apartment and hope it comes out clean."

"I have let this place go." Looking around, Joshua grimaced. "Maybe if I clean this place up, they'll let me stay."

Juan Carlos shook his head. "I'll get a cleaning crew to come in and do that, but I'm keeping you close for the time being. There's an empty three-bedroom luxury apartment at DJC Towers."

Juan Carlos put his phone to his ear. "Hello, Diego. I need your help. I'm going to move Joshua into that empty three-bedroom apartment in DJC, but he needs two roommates we can trust to keep an eye on him." Juan Carlos paused. "Okay."

"Who?" Juan Carlos asked. Juan Carlos shook his head. "Was there another Code Diego?" Juan Carlos sighed. "Fine. Hasta después." Juan Carlos hung up his phone. "We're going to get you moved in right away." Juan Carlos motioned around the room. "Is there anything here you want, that you think we can salvage?"

Joshua shook his head. "No." Joshua stood, sending an avalanche of clothes off the couch, knocking into the coffee table. A tube of lipstick fell over and began rolling off the edge. Joshua quickly snapped it up.

"What is that?" Juan Carlos asked curiously.

Joshua held the tube protectively in his hand. "Lipstick."

"I didn't know you wore makeup." Juan Carlos smiled.

Joshua stared at his hand for a moment, then opened it. "I don't." He handed the lipstick to Juan Carlos. "A couple of months ago, I was in the woods looking for Teddy. I found it at his cave."

"Teddy, as in one of the Three Bears that kidnapped you?" Juan Carlos clarified.

Joshua nodded. "He wasn't like the other two. He was nice, and we had a real connection. He was trying to find a way to fix that Build and Burn shit."

"Okay," Juan Carlos said cautiously. "Go on."

Joshua scratched at his head. "His cave was ransacked. It looked like there was some type of fight." Joshua pointed to the lipstick. "I found that there."

"Murderous Red." Juan Carlos read the tube's name out loud. "I don't think I've ever heard of this shade. What else can you tell me about what happened in the woods?"

Joshua sat down. "I didn't find Teddy's cave. I actually fell and hit my head. Jack found me and nursed me back to health." He looked up at Juan Carlos with watery eyes. "He took me to Teddy's cave. We've been trying to find him for months."

"You and Jack?" Juan Carlos put a hand on his shoulder. "Who is this Jack?"

Joshua shook his head. "He told me he was Teddy's boyfriend. I guess he's sort of mine now, too, or was."

"What happened?" Juan Carlos asked with concern.

Joshua closed his eyes. "We had a fight because he was going to follow up on a lead on Teddy, and he didn't want me coming along because it was dangerous. When I refused, he kicked me out of the woods."

"Kicked you out of the woods?" Juan Carlos asked, confused.

Joshua chuckled softly. "Yeah, Jack is, well, you wouldn't believe me if I told you."

"Try me." Juan Carlos smirked. "I've seen and heard a lot in my time."

Joshua shrugged. "Okay. Jack has two dads. One is human, the other is a Drus. Don't ask me how Jack was conceived, but he's part Drus." Shaking his head, Joshua looked at Juan Carlos. "You don't believe me? Do you?"

"Oh, I believe you," Juan Carlos said reassuringly. "Remind me to take you to In Between so I can introduce you to Ryuu. He's an asexual dragon dating a unicorn."

Joshua scoffed. "You're making fun of me."

"I'm completely serious. I also met an actual fairy named Jase." Juan Carlos extended his hand out. "Come on, let's get you cleaned up, and I'll tell you all about it."

CHAPTER 5

DIEGO MARVELED AT HOW THE young man sitting in front of him looked so much like his brother but was so radically different. The ends of Aiden's hair were tipped in bright red. His clothes were vibrant and colorful, and his smile looked playful yet serious. Then there was his carefree attitude.

"Why do you want to be Mr. Sanz's personal assistant?" Alex asked from beside Diego.

With a casual air in his voice, Aiden answered, "I don't. You want me." Aiden focused his attention on Alex. "You're the boyfriend? Here to make sure I don't try to steal your man?"

"Yes, err, no," Alex stumbled. "I am his boyfriend, but I'm not worried about you stealing him."

Aiden's body shook with a quiet chuckle. "You don't have to worry about me. Diego isn't my type."

"Because I'm a daddy. I know," Diego groaned.

Aiden cocked his head quizzically at Diego. "Who told you that? You're not a daddy, you're a hot papi."

"Isn't that the same thing?" Alex asked, confused.

Diego put a hand on Alex's leg. "No, because he put hot in front of it."

"A hot papi can be any age," Aiden clarified. "Not like wolves or twinks."

Alex groaned, "I'm so out of touch."

"Don't worry, I'll teach you when we hang out." Aiden smiled.

Relieved, Alex said, "Thank you." Then Alex registered what Aiden said. "Wait. Who said we're hanging out?"

"Come on, the boss's boyfriend and his personal assistant?" Aiden grinned. "We were destined to be besties."

Bewildered, Diego jumped in, "Hold on. Who said we're offering you the job?"

"Who said I'm accepting it?" Aiden countered. Confidently, Aiden crossed his legs. "I have some demands."

Diego raised an eyebrow in bewilderment. "Demands?"

"Yes." Aiden waved a finger between the two. "First off, no sex in the office, and if you do have sex, I'm not cleaning it up."

Flustered, Alex sputtered, "We don't have sex in the office."

"Sure." Aiden winked at him. "Second, I'm all for fun in the office, but you're going to get your work done. Third, when I'm off work, I'm off. Don't be calling me after work or coming downstairs to my apartment to get me to order you a pizza or prepare you for a meeting."

Alex looked at Diego, then at Aiden. "Wait. What does he mean, 'coming downstairs to his apartment?'"

"He and Aspen are taking the vacant apartment in DJC Tower with Joshua," Diego explained. He then quickly added, "It was Juan Carlos's idea."

Aiden smirked. "Lastly, no popping by to hang out." He pointed at Alex. "He can, but Diego can't."

"Right, work-life balance." Diego nodded.

Aiden made a face. "No, my brother admires you. He idolizes you, how you're wild, crazy, smart, yet so cool and collected. He's jealous that you've got that balance and he doesn't."

"Aspen?" Alex and Diego blurted out in disbelief.

Aiden laughed. "Don't let his icy demeanor fool you. He's passionate. He doesn't really know how to show it safely."

"I'd like to see it," Diego grumbled. "He's always cold to me."

Aiden pursed his lips. "Yeah, that's how you can tell he likes you."

"Well, he's mine," Alex said possessively.

Aiden put up a hand. "Diego isn't his type. He likes guys around his age. Diego is, well, vintage as far as Aspen is concerned."

"Now I feel old," Diego sulked.

Alex put a hand on his shoulder. "You're not old." He grinned. "You're vintage."

"Okay, I'm feeling this vibe. What time do I start tomorrow?" Aiden asked.

"Eight." Diego shook his head. "Am I going to regret this?"

"I have a feeling I'm going to love this." Alex laughed.

Aiden stood. "Oh, one last thing. I want a balcony at the apartment."

CHAPTER 6

JOSHUA DIDN'T RECOGNIZE HIM-self in the full-length mirror of his new bed-room. His sandy blond hair was trimmed down and his curls hung neatly around his head. The scraggly beard was gone, letting the world see his cherub baby face. Except his face wasn't cherubic any longer. It was thin and angular. His body was trim and hard from living and training with Jack.

He wasn't the optimistic young man that was kidnapped. He wasn't the sugar bear that flirted with Teddy in that gym. He wasn't the deter-mined and hopeful man that ventured out into the woods. He was an angry, defeated, and bitter man who had lost hope for love that wanted to hide away from the world.

Joshua pulled on a powder blue polo and then a pair of jeans that hugged his body. Juan Carlos bought these clothes for him, along with the rest that were in his closet and drawers. Juan Carlos also paid for the haircut, pedicure, manicure, and the multitude of hair, skin, and bath products. "An emergency makeover," he had called it.

Joshua left his room and headed down the hall past the two empty rooms waiting for his roommates. He stepped into the living room, where Juan Carlos waited for him on the couch. Joshua found himself being self-conscious about his appearance when Juan Carlos stood and smiled at him.

"Don't you look spectacular?" Juan Carlos beamed.

Joshua shifted from foot to foot. "Thanks." He smiled at Juan Carlos. "For everything."

"It was my pleasure." Juan Carlos adjusted his collar. He took Joshua's hands. "What are your feelings on the nail polish? I know you were resistant at first, but that blue looks great on you."

Joshua fought the urge to pull his hands away. "I like it," he admitted. "I'm going to keep it for now."

"Great!" Juan Carlos patted him on the chest. "Your roommate, Aiden, is on his way up."

Joshua felt his stomach twist into knots. "Do you know what he's like?"

"Not a clue." Juan Carlos shrugged. "I know his brother Aspen. He's a lovely young man. Very quiet and reserved. I imagine that his brother can't be much different."

Nervously, Joshua asked, "Do you think they'll be mad that I took the room with a balcony?"

"Not at all." Juan Carlos took Joshua's hand and led him over to the couch. "Now remember, the three of you are having dinner with us in the penthouse."

Joshua relaxed, but only for a moment. Juan Carlos gave him so much and asked for nothing in return. He trusted Juan Carlos with the truth about Jack. He knew he could trust Juan Carlos with the truth about Build and Burn. Juan Carlos was at the top of DJC. He could do something about it, and maybe help him find Teddy. Joshua was about to confide in him when Aiden made his entrance.

"Oh! My! God!" Aiden proclaimed, exploding into the apartment. "This place is fabulous!" He paused to look around. "It could use a bit of color, but that's why you have me!"

Aiden rushed to Joshua and Juan Carlos. He grabbed Joshua's hand. "You must be Joshua!" He looked at Juan Carlos. "You, I have no idea who you could be." Aiden rushed to the small terrace patio. "Oh, this is the perfect spot for me to read!"

"Does he have an off switch?" Joshua whispered to Juan Carlos.

Juan Carlos whispered back, "I hope so. He's nothing like his brother."

"Sorry!" Aiden rushed back over to Juan Carlos and Joshua. "I'm a bit excited! This place is wonderful!" Aiden bounced on his heels. "Where is my room? It's the one with the balcony."

Joshua looked at Juan Carlos before awkwardly saying, "That's my room."

"Diego said I could have it." Aiden gave him a wink. "You can come in anytime and use it, though."

Juan Carlos cleared his throat. "He gets the balcony. You and Aspen have the other two rooms."

"Who are you exactly?" Aiden asked, crossing his arms and tapping his foot.

Juan Carlos smiled wickedly. "Juan Carlos Sanz. Perhaps you've heard of me."

"The one they told me not to cross in HR?" Aiden asked, his eyes growing wide. "The stories I've heard. I don't know whether to be afraid or in awe of you."

Juan Carlos said proudly, "Both."

"Fair." Aiden nodded. "Okay, he can have the balcony, but I get the decorating power of this room."

Feeling a bit relieved, Joshua said, "Yeah, you and Aspen can do what you like with the place."

"Great." Aiden plopped down in the loveseat. "Tell me about yourself. What are your hopes? Your dreams? What do you do?"

Juan Carlos pulled Joshua down onto the couch with him. "There will be time for all that later. First, we have to go over the rules of the apartment."

"Rules?" Aiden laughed. "I'm a grown..." He trailed off when he saw Juan Carlos's stern glare. "Rules. I can do rules."

Juan Carlos patted Joshua's knee. "Loud music in your rooms only. The walls are sound-proof. Everyone keeps this place clean. Sunday brunch is up at the penthouse. You and Aspen are welcome to join. Joshua is coming to dinner tonight in the penthouse. Again, you and Aspen are welcome to join. You might as well, since I'm telling you that you're required to come."

"Hhmm," Aiden thought. "Okay. Can I have boys in my room?"

Juan Carlos laughed. "I said the walls are soundproof."

Aiden popped up off the couch. "Great. The movers are downstairs waiting on me. Is there a storage unit that I can put Aspen's furniture in?"

Aiden looked around. "His stuff is nice, but not nearly as nice as this stuff."

"Ask the person at the front desk," Juan Carlos answered. "The storage units are in the sub-basement."

Aiden looked toward the hall. "I guess I should claim my room." He rushed down the hallway and into one of the vacant rooms. "This is huge! Is that a bay window?! This high up?!" He rushed across to the other room. "Is that a hideaway dedicated workspace? That is perfect for Aspen's gaming systems!"

Aiden popped out of the room. "Keep the balcony. These rooms are perfect for us!"

"Good." Juan Carlos smiled. "If you need anything, I'm right upstairs."

Aiden looked as if he were going to burst from the excitement. "Okay, I'm going to get our stuff!" He rushed out of the apartment, leaving Juan Carlos and Joshua shaking their heads.

"Wow. Is he always on a ten?" Joshua asked.

"I sure hope not," Juan Carlos answered. "He's nothing like his twin brother."

Stunned, Joshua blurted out, "There's two of them?!"

"Don't worry. Aspen isn't so flamboyant." Juan Carlos patted his leg. "If you ever need to get away, you can come up and sit in my garden."

Joshua laughed. "Thank you. If he gets to be too much, I'll just sit on him."

"You got to catch him first." Juan Carlos stood. "I need to get dinner started. I'm upstairs if you need me."

Joshua relaxed back into the couch. Juan Carlos had barely left when Joshua jumped up, remembering he needed to tell Juan Carlos what he knew about Build and Burn. The moment he opened the door, Aiden came through. Aiden bounced off Joshua's firm toned body, landing on his butt and sending the boxes he was carrying flying about.

"I'm so sorry." Joshua offered Aiden a hand. "Are you okay?"

Aiden took the offered hand. "No, harm. No, foul." Getting back to his feet, Aiden asked, "Where were you heading off to?"

"I forgot to tell Juan Carlos something." Joshua felt guilty. "I hope I didn't break anything." He leaned down and started picking up boxes. "I'll pay for anything I broke."

Aiden started gathering his things. He dismissed Joshua's worries. "These are just boxes of clothes and shoes."

"Do you need any help bringing anything up?" Joshua offered, walking with Aiden to his room.

Aiden stepped ahead of Joshua and headed into the room he claimed. "Nope. The movers Diego sent are bringing the rest up. This was just what I brought in my car." Setting the boxes down, Aiden spun around the room. "This place is so nice!"

"Yes, it is." Joshua set his boxes down by the others.

Noticing Joshua's nails, Aiden took his hand. "I love your polish! We are so giving each other manicures!"

"I, uh, don't know how to," Joshua admitted shyly. "Juan Carlos talked me into it."

"I'll teach you." Aiden patted Joshua's hand. "I know I can be too much sometimes. When I am, tell me. I won't be offended."

Pulling his hand back, Joshua said, "I doubt I'll mind, but I will if I need to."

"Good." Aiden jumped up and down. "I can't believe this place is ours!"

Joshua smiled. "You're going to be trouble, aren't you?"

"Yes, and you're going to love it." Aiden gave him a playful smile.

CHAPTER 7

GAYMER ADJUSTED THE ZOOM ON his goggles. He peered down into the small electronic box, soldering wires and fuses. His uncle, Mayor Trainer, wanted to boost the power of his little toy. It didn't matter that Gaymer had told him that it wouldn't work. The signal degraded the farther it went out, no matter how much power you pumped into it. He was able to boost the range to twelve feet, but even that was pushing the limits of the device.

"Aren't you done yet?" Mayor Trainer growled impatiently at him.

Setting the soldering iron aside, Gaymer pushed the goggles to the top of his head. "I told you, this isn't going to work. What you need is a bunch of these boxes all over the city, and we don't have the resources to do that."

"Have some respect," Brutus barked from beside Mayor Trainer. "Impotent little brat."

Gaymer sneered at Brutus. "Does somebody need to go for his walkies?"

"Easy, Brutus." Mayor Trainer put up an arm to stop him from attacking his nephew. "Victor—"

"Gaymer," he corrected.

Mayor Trainer nodded. "Gaymer, we need this one to reach the entire city. Now make it happen."

"If I push its range any farther, it's going to short out." Gaymer stood to face the two men. "I looked at the programming. It wasn't designed to work more than six feet like the ones you have in your basement puppy pound." Gaymer smirked at his uncle's discomfort. "Yeah, Uncle Doug, I know your little secret."

Through gritted teeth, Brutus pleaded, "Let me slap the shit off him one time."

"Down boy," Mayor Trainer ordered. "Gaymer, what does or does not happen in my basement is none of your concern. What is your concern," Mayor Trainer shouted, "is to get that box to work like I told you I want it to!"

Gaymer snorted. "I can boost the signal like you want, but it's not going to work."

"You'll make it work, or else," Brutus snarled, body tensed and ready to strike.

Gaymer pretended to yawn. "Down, Fido, or I'll have you neutered."

"Enough! Both of you!" Mayor Trainer shouted. "Brutus, go check on our new recruits. I'll handle Gaymer."

"Yes, sir." Brutus stomped out of the office, nostrils flaring.

Gaymer rolled his eyes. "You really should look into obedience training for him."

"I said, enough!" Mayor Trainer stood. "Get that device up and working like I told you and stop antagonizing Brutus!"

Gaymer unplugged the soldering iron. Snippily, he announced, "I need to get some more parts. I'll be back in a bit." He glared at his uncle. "Make sure your puppy is on his leash when I get back."

"Be back within the hour!" Mayor Trainer shouted at Gaymer's back as he left.

Stepping out onto the sidewalk, Gaymer fumed. *Idiots. Just because they want it to work a certain way doesn't mean it can!* Gaymer turned the corner and headed to his favorite comic book store. *If I don't get the latest copy of* The Moon Prince *because they wanted me to screw around.* Gamer huffed.

After power walking the next two blocks, Gaymer felt the rage leave his body when he saw the sign for Cosmic Moon Comics in the distance. He dodged through the business people filling the sidewalks on their way to eat their lunches. Opening the door to the shop, Gaymer paused. He spotted a man he had to know.

Gaymer wasn't normally into the clean-cut business type, but this slender man had a style that demanded Gaymer's attention. The heels of his shiny black shoes clacked on the pavement. His black dress pants had a thin white stripe up the side of each leg. The only splash of color was a silvery blue tie that matched the highlights in his blond hair.

"Thank you," Aspen said, walking through the door Gaymer was holding open.

Gaymer followed him in, grateful the man looked as good going as he did coming. "Damn," Gaymer said to himself. He slipped between the isles, heading to *The Moon Prince* display while surreptitiously watching the eye-catching young man making his way to the same display. Gaymer smiled at Aspen as he reached for the last copy the very moment Aspen did.

"A Little Prince fan, too?" Gaymer asked, tugging the comic toward him.

Aspen pulled the comic back toward him. "Yes, and I'd like to go and complete my purchase now."

"Sorry, but I had it first." Gaymer tugged it back.

Aspen tugged it back. His voice was frosty when he spoke. "I had it first. Now, if you don't mind, I'm on my lunch break and don't have time for your nonsense."

"I do mind because I'm having a really bad day and I've been looking forward to this comic all day." Gaymer cracked a mischievous smile at Aspen. "I could be persuaded to relinquish my claim if I had something else to brighten my day."

Aspen looked at Gaymer, taking in his low-hung jeans, graphic tee, multicolor hair, and goggles on the top of his head. "What?"

"A date." Gaymer snatched the comic out of Aspen's hands.

Aspen's eyes grew cold. "Give that back."

"Give me a date," Gaymer said playfully. "I'm Gaymer, by the way."

Aspen narrowed his eyes at Gaymer. "IceQween25." Aspen then added, "My gamer screen name. I'm Aspen."

"Oh, I'm Gaymer68." He winked at Aspen. "You're not getting this," he waved the comic in front of Aspen, "unless I get your number."

Aspen chuffed in annoyance. "Fine, it's—"

"Nope," Gaymer cut him off. "Hand me your phone unlocked and I'll call myself from it so I know it's the real number."

Aspen pulled his phone out and unlocked it. "Same time." He passed the comic over at the same time Aspen took the phone. "Thank you."

"You're welcome." Gaymer quickly typed away into Aspen's phone. "I'll be on at nine tonight. Let's team up."

Aspen snatched his phone back. "You know I'm going to block your number the moment I leave here."

"You would if you could." Gaymer smiled. "I programmed your phone to accept my calls even if you block it. Never give a hacker your phone." Gaymer winked at him. "I'll talk to you later, Aspen." He walked away, content with his prize.

CHAPTER 8

"ALEX, CAN YOU FIX MY PHONE?" an exasperated Aspen asked, entering his office.

Alex looked up from his screen and smiled. "Sure. What is it? A broken screen? Loose charging port?"

"No." Aspen handed his phone over. "I think it's a virus or malware."

Taking the phone, Alex stood. "Let me hook it up to my isolation console, then. We don't want to infect the entire system by accident." He plugged the phone into the console. "We have enough chaos around here as it is."

"Tell me about it." Aspen leaned against the desk. "How can you put up with it?"

Alex started the scan, then looked up at Aiden quizzically. "Put up with what?"

"Diego and his antics, for one," Aspen groaned, shaking his head. "Like last week when he had Dion riding some motorized inline skates, making her late for a videoconference."

Alex laughed. "She did it because it was fun. As proper as Dion portrays herself around here, she loves Diego's antics. It keeps this place from being boring, and those skates weren't what she was helping test. It was the safety gear she was wearing. "

Aspen thought for a moment. "She wasn't wearing any safety gear."

"None that you saw. That was the point." The computer beeped. Alex turned to it. Reading the screen, he said, "Interesting. There's no virus, malware, or ransomware on your phone."

Aspen looked at the screen. "There has to be something. That damn timer keeps popping up on my phone."

"This?" Alex held up the phone for Aspen to see. "What's it for?"

Through gritted teeth, Aspen said, "Yes. Some degenerate at Cosmic Moon Comics made me hand him my phone to put his number in so he'd let go of my copy of *The Moon Prince*."

"Would his name be Gaymer?" Alex asked, looking at the phone. He handed the phone back to Aspen. "He sent you a message."

Taking the phone, Aspen read the message out loud:

[The timer is counting down until tonight when we can team up.]

"Team up?" Alex asked, curiously. "What does that mean?"

Handing the phone back to Alex, Aspen answered, "Online gaming. My handle is IceQween25."

"So, you have a date?" Alex grinned. "Are you going to keep it?"

Aspen made a dismissive sound. "No."

"Liar," Alex challenged. "Tell the truth or I'll tell Diego you have a love interest." Aspen's eyes grew wide. "You've heard those stories, haven't you?"

Aspen scowled at Alex. "I thought you were a friend."

"I am. Your brother says he and I are going to be besties." Alex beamed. "I could tell him about your little date."

Aspen pushed himself off the desk. "Jerk." Aspen clenched his fists and let out a sound of frustration. "Why am I always attracted to guys that infuriate me?"

"Maybe because they remind you to cut loose and have fun, and you enjoy reigning in their craziness," Alex offered.

Aspen shook his head no, but said, "You're absolutely right." He faced Alex. "Diego drives me bonkers, but I love every minute of it."

"You know he's my boyfriend," Alex reminded him. "You're not going to be the next Code Diego, are you?"

Offended, Aspen proclaimed, "No! He's vintage. He's hot and all, but he's like…"

"A daddy?" Alex finished. "Aiden calls him a hot papi."

"He would," Aspen snipped.

Alex motioned to the spare chair. "Tell me about this Gaymer guy you met at Cosmic Moon Comics."

"I don't know much other than he's an arrogant guy with multicolored hair that dresses like he's still in high school," Aspen said, taking a seat. "The thing is, I want to get to know him. That stunt he pulled in the store…" He clenched and unclenched his hands. "It drove me crazy, but I enjoyed it. Which made me angry at myself."

Leaning against the desk, Alex crossed his ankles. "Why were you mad at yourself?"

"Because," Aspen made a fist, "what he did was unexpected. It threw off my schedule and my routine."

Alex grinned. "And you liked it."

"Yes!" Aspen exclaimed. "Why?"

Alex gave Aspen a sympathetic look. "Because it was unexpected. It was a bit of excitement. It took you out of your comfort zone, and you needed that."

"I don't need that," Aspen countered. "My brother loves that, but not me."

Alex snickered. "Yes, you do. We all do, even if it's a little bit. Why do you think Diego and I mesh so well? He's wild and crazy. I'm his anchor. Sure, he drags me along sometimes, but in the end, I'm better for it, and have some great stories."

"What do I do about this?" Aspen asked, waving his phone around.

Alex felt the spirit of Juan Carlos in him. "You keep that date and see where it goes. Give Gaymer a chance. What time is your date with him tonight?"

"Nine," Aspen sighed.

Alex shrugged. "I'll make sure we're done with dinner by then."

"Thanks." Aspen stood. "Wait, what was that about dinner?"

Alex bit his lower lip. "Juan Carlos sent a text saying you guys were coming to dinner tonight."

"Could this day get any worse?" Aspen groaned.

"Hey, Alex, I—" Diego came into the lab. "Oh, Aspen, hey. Am I interrupting?'

Alex saw the warning look Aspen shot him. "Aspen needed me to look at his phone. He was just leaving."

"Don't go." Diego smiled mischievously. "R and D just sent up the prototype of the exoskeleton suits. You can help us test them."

Aspen tensed. "I'm good. My schedule has been disrupted enough today." He nodded to both of them politely and said, "Gentlemen," before walking to the door.

"See you at dinner tonight!" Diego called after him.

Aspen paused and smiled politely back at him. "Yes, I guess you will." Before leaving, he looked at Alex and said, "Remember your promise."

CHAPTER 9

MAYOR TRAINER WATCHED THE young man in the isolation room writhing on the floor from the window in the door. The young man was foolishly struggling against the hypno-box's control that crept into his subconscious. The fight was futile. The hypno-box used a high-frequency sound that slipped into the minds of the person before they knew it was happening.

"He and the other five will be ready soon," Brutus said, walking up. "Do you want to name them now or later?"

Turning to Brutus, Mayor Trainer said, "I'll name them when we return. You have to get back to the police station and handle the fallout of the Three Pigs' accidental deaths. I need to get to the mayor's office and prepare a statement."

"Then it's done?" Brutus asked, a slight hint of worry in his voice.

"It will be by the time you get there." Mayor Trainer sighed.

Brutus's brows furrowed. "How's it going to happen?"

"I don't know, and I don't care." Mayor Trainer patted Brutus on the shoulder. "I've already sent you a copy of the statement we're going to release to the press."

Brutus nodded. "Yes, sir. What about Gaymer? Shouldn't one of us keep an eye on him?"

"Don't worry about him. He knows not to bite the hand that feeds him." Mayor Trainer dismissed his fears. "Come, we have political rivals to publically destroy."

Brutus followed Mayor Trainer out of the basement. "Do you think this will boost our approval ratings?"

"Of course. If not, we'll have the souped-up hypno-box Gaymer is working on." Mayor Trainer turned to face Brutus. "As soon as they inform you, I want your first call to be to me."

Stoically, Brutus answered, "Yes, sir."

"Let me look at you." Mayor Trainer adjusted Brutus's collar and straightened his pins. "Make sure you look your best on camera. I want them to get good pictures of you."

A smile cracked Brutus's stone features. "Of course, sir."

"Tonight, we'll lay in bed together and watch as our poll numbers skyrocket." Mayor Trainer lightly kissed Brutus on the lips. "Then we can celebrate."

Brutus's smile broadened. "I like it when we celebrate."

"I do, too." Mayor Trainer's voice was low and seductive. "When we win this election, we'll announce our relationship and start planning our wedding."

Brutus looked at him in confusion. "Our wedding?"

"Yes." Mayor Trainer pulled out a small ring box and dropped to one knee. Opening the box, he presented the ring to Brutus. "Brutus Howard, will you marry me?"

Brutus trembled with emotion. "I wear your collar proudly, and I'll do the same with your ring." He reached out for the ring, but Mayor Trainer pulled it from the box and slipped the golden band onto Brutus's finger.

"I will protect you and cherish you." Holding Brutus's hand, Mayor Trainer stood. "I want you as my Pup, my partner, and my husband."

Squeezing Mayor Trainer's hands, Brutus said, "You've made me the happiest Pup in the world. I'll love and protect you until the end of my days."

"With you as police chief and me as mayor for another term, we'll rule this city." Mayor Trainer ran a hand over Brutus's shiny black scalp. "Go now. We have work to do. I'm going to check on Gaymer and I'll be right behind you."

Brutus visibly bristled at the mention of Gaymer's name. "If he wasn't your nephew."

"I'll talk to him." Mayor Trainer kissed him one last time. "Now, go. Time is of the essence to stay ahead of this."

"What do you think you're doing?" Mayor Trainer shouted when he found Gaymer with his feet on the desk, reclining in his chair.

Gaymer opened a sleepy eye. "Taking a nap."

"You can nap when you're done!" Mayor Trainer knocked his feet off the desk. "Do you think this is one of your stupid online games?"

Gaymer jumped to his feet. "No. What I think is that you aren't listening to me when I tell you that you can have it work or you can have the range you want. You can't have both." Gaymer wasn't going to let his uncle's six-foot-six height intimidate him. At five foot five, he was used to standing up to the bigger guys. "Sound deteriorates the farther it travels from its source, and modern recording equipment is designed to filter out erroneous sounds. It simply won't work."

"Fine." Mayor Trainer gritted his perfectly white teeth. "What about making it smaller, then? Something a person could carry around?"

Gaymer thought for a second. "Yeah, it would drive the person mad if they were subjected to the signal for too long."

"Could you make something that could block the signal for the person carrying it around?" Mayor Trainer asked, an idea forming in his head. "Something that wouldn't be noticeable to the human eye?"

Gaymer scrunched his face in thought. "Yeah, I guess. It's just a matter of blocking a sound wave."

"Good." Mayor Trainer grinned. "I want at least thirty by tomorrow."

Gaymer let out a laugh. "You can want, but you're not going to get. First, I have to design and test the prototypes. You've got at least twenty-four hours before I can mass produce them."

"Fine." Mayor Trainer huffed in annoyance. "I'm off to the office to handle an upcoming crisis. Clean up and then let yourself out."

Gaymer raised an eyebrow. "Upcoming crisis?"

"Nothing you need to worry about, dear nephew," Mayor Trainer said smugly. "Oh, and stop antagonizing Brutus. I will not have you disrespecting my future husband."

"Future husband? Congratulations." Gaymer rolled his eyes. He hugged his uncle. "I'll make an effort to be nicer to him."

Mayor Trainer smiled. "Thank you. I'll check on your progress later."

CHAPTER 10

"QUIT SULKING AND GO MINGLE with everyone." Alex put a hand on the brooding Aspen's shoulder. "You're going to be here on a regular basis, anyways, with Sunday brunch, so you might as well get used to it."

Aspen's eyes narrowed. "Sunday brunch? I have to come back up here for Sunday brunch, too?"

"It's a family thing," Alex responded. "Like it or not, you're part of the family now."

Aspen covered his face with his hand. "Could this get any worse?"

"Aspen!" Aiden shouted. "Come check out this garden! I could read for hours out there!"

From the kitchen, Juan Carlos shouted, "Use it anytime you like!"

"Within reason!" Diego quickly added. "We do like our privacy."

Aspen looked at Alex. "I'll make sure he doesn't make a pest of himself."

"Your place is amazing, Alex," Joshua said, walking up.

Alex quickly corrected him, "I don't live here. This is Juan Carlos's and Diego's place. I have my own place in Northside."

"That he rarely ever stays in anymore," Diego said, coming up and putting an arm around Alex. "Maybe you two can finally convince him to move in here with me."

Alex hip-bumped Diego. "I'm not ready for that yet. I like having my own place."

"He likes having a place of his own he can escape to, just like me," Aaron said, joining the group.

Salaciously, Diego growled, "He'll never escape me."

"Diego," Alex playfully chided. "We have company."

Aaron laughed. "Like that matters? Remember when he asked me if I was going to be his daddy?"

"I heard," Aspen groaned. "I believe some of the first paperwork I had to do was a result of that conversation."

Popping up alongside Aspen, Aiden asked, "What are we talking about?"

"You are just a bouncy thing, aren't you?" Aaron asked.

Aiden winked at him. "Most people call me a firecracker."

"Dinner is served!" Juan Carlos announced, coming out of the kitchen with a steaming dish and Felipe right behind him. "We have a traditional lasagna made with a special sauce you all are going to love."

Setting two covered baskets on the table, Felipe announced, "We have plenty of garlic and cheese bread."

"Sit! Everyone, sit!" Juan Carlos motioned to everyone. "I got this recipe from a very dear and sweet friend."

Sitting down, Diego amended, "That means they dated."

"Oh, Antonio. The best thing about him was his cooking," Juan Carlos mused.

Taking the seat next to Diego, Alex patted the seat next to him. "Sit next to me, Aspen." He winked. "It's safer. Out of his line of sight."

"Thank you." Aspen sat down. He smiled across the table at his brother. "Are all meals here so elaborate?"

Aaron pecked Juan Carlos's cheek before sitting down. "I wish. Normally, this is reserved for Sunday brunch."

"Even Dion comes for Sunday dinners." Diego grinned. "She'd be here now, but she has a date."

The table went silent. Uncomfortably, Alex cleared his throat. "How do you know about her date?"

"I—" Diego started before Juan Carlos cut him off.

"What did you do?" Juan Carlos fixed his stern glare on Diego. "I swear, Diego, if you ruin her date, I will put you over my knee and live stream it for the world to see."

Before Diego could respond, Alex accused, "You hacked her phone, didn't you?"

"At least I have Aiden to help me with the paperwork now," Aspen lamented.

Aiden raised his hand. "Excuse me. Am I missing something?"

"HR didn't tell you?" Joshua asked. "They made me watch a video about the dangers of telling Diego you're interested in someone." Joshua thought for a moment. "I think it was called, 'No, Diego, No!'"

"If I—" Diego started, but was promptly cut off.

"We have our own version of a Code Diego at the police station," Aaron groaned, pulling out his phone. "I should give them a heads up."

Felipe pulled out his phone. "Good idea. I should give my campaign manager a heads up."

"Diego, how could you? This is her first date in months," Alex scolded, shaking his head.

Raising his voice, Diego proclaimed, "I didn't do anything!" Everyone at the table grew quiet. "Okay, I did set Dion up on the date, but I didn't do anything to help it."

"Who did you set her up with?" Juan Carlos asked, suspiciously.

Meekly, Diego answered, "Demona Angel."

"What?!" Alex and Juan Carlos shouted.

Aaron shook his head. "I don't even know who to call to clean that one up."

"You don't have to call anyone. Demona saw a picture of me and Dion on my phone and she asked me to introduce her to Dion," Diego explained, trying to act innocent.

Alex hung his head down. "I have a feeling this isn't going to turn out good."

"Diego, does Dion know that Demona is..." Juan Carlos paused to choose his next words, "...a bar owner?"

Smugly, Diego said, "I didn't think it was my place to out her as ... a bar owner."

"I don't get it," Aiden spoke up. "What's the big deal about her being a bar owner?"

Juan Carlos exchanged a quick glance with Diego before answering, "She owns In Between.

Not really the type of establishment Dion would frequent."

"What's the big deal about the bar?" Joshua asked, genuinely curious.

Juan Carlos cautiously answered, "It's the special bar I told you about."

"Oh!" Joshua exclaimed.

Shocked, Alex looked over at Juan Carlos. "He knows about In Between?!"

"And you thought I was the bad one at the table." Diego laughed softly.

Holding up his phone, Felipe asked, "Am I calling my campaign manager or not?"

"No!" Juan Carlos and Diego shouted simultaneously.

In his icy tone, Aspen asked, "Can we eat now?"

After dinner, Joshua helped Juan Carlos and Aaron with the dishes, letting Aiden, Aspen, Felipe, Alex, and Diego retire outside to enjoy the peacefulness of the garden. The lights of the city were slowly replacing the light of the setting sun. Under the shade of the banana trees, Esmerelda's wolf flowers began to open.

"Okay, I got to know," Aiden spoke up, breaking the silence. "How are Diego and Felipe related? You two are brothers, but look nothing alike."

Felipe smiled. "Juan Carlos is my father. Long story." He pointed at Diego. "Juan Carlos adopted him. That's why we have the same father."

"Juan Carlos isn't my father," Diego corrected him. "He's my mamacita."

Alex chimed in, "And Juan Carlos didn't adopt Diego, legally. Diego just changed his last name."

"Wait. What?" Felipe asked, bewildered. "I thought he adopted you."

Diego shook his head. "No, he took me in and raised me. He taught me everything I know."

"Wait, all the information about you two." Felipe pulled out his phone. "They said Juan Carlos adopted you as his own."

Aiden laughed. "Creative writing. It's not what you say, but how you say it."

"I really should be getting downstairs," Aspen announced, checking the time on his phone.

Aaron came rushing out, followed by Juan Carlos and Joshua. "Felipe, we need to go. The Three Pigs were found dead in their jail cell and Mayor Trainer and Chief Brutus are bashing us in their press conference."

"By the time we get on the air, it'll be too late," Felipe said, standing. "Assholes."

Alex thought for a moment. "All we need is a location, a camera, and someone to do your hair and makeup."

"We have all that, and I can link the feed to the news agency," Diego added.

Confused, Felipe asked, "What exactly are we doing?"

"You're holding your press conference here in my garden." Juan Carlos grinned. "I've always wanted to do my son's makeup."

Overwhelmed, Felipe said, "Okay, but what about Aaron?"

"We've got stuff that will match his skin tone." Aspen stood. "Come on, Aiden."

Jumping up, Aiden exclaimed, "And you thought tonight was going to be boring!"

Joshua sat the stack of dishes in the sink. Juan Carlos gave him an appreciative smile. Looking at Aaron wrapping up the meager leftovers, Joshua worried his lip. He wasn't sure how to broach the subject of Teddy, or if Aaron knew about the mythical community. If he could only get Juan Carlos alone.

"Dimelo." Juan Carlos put a gentle hand on Joshua's arm.

Startled, Joshua said, "I don't speak Spanish."

"You'll pick up on it," Aaron commented. "He wants to know what's on your mind."

Joshua looked at Aaron, then cautiously asked, "How much does he know about, you know, In Between?"

"Everything," Aaron answered, bringing over the casserole dish. "I play cards with a group of gnomes."

Joshua visibly relaxed. "Then it's okay to talk about Jack being a Drus."

"Oh, absolutely." Juan Carlos returned to rinsing the dishes in the sink. "The only people here that don't know are Felipe, Aiden, and Aspen. What's on your mind?"

Nervously, Joshua said, "It's about Teddy. I meant to tell you earlier, but Aiden came in." Juan Carlos and Aaron stopped what they were doing to give him their full attention. "Before that Shadow Guardian dude came, Teddy was changing. For the better," Joshua quickly clarified. "He wasn't using the same Build and Burn the other two were using. He was using the stuff he made." Joshua swallowed hard. "As you know, he went into the woods, and that's where Jack found him."

"Wait, who's Jack?" Aaron asked.

Joshua bit the inside of his cheek. "He's the Drus I met, well, half Drus. He's Teddy's boyfriend and sort of mine." Joshua let out a humorless laugh. "It's complicated, but anyways. He found Teddy and helped purge this thing out of him. Something that the Build and Burn was feeding. Jack called it a 'Rage Seed.' It was growing inside him."

"That makes sense, sort of," Juan Carlos commented. "Esmerelda said there was something mystical about it, but she couldn't pin it down."

Joshua continued, "That's because it's not mystical until it finds a host. Then it grows quickly, and it eats away at the person, turning them into mad powerful creatures."

"You said Jack purged it out of Teddy," Aaron stated. "How is he now?"

Defeated, Joshua said, "I don't know. When Jack found me, someone had already tracked down Teddy and taken him. Our only clue was that lipstick." Joshua's eyes grew wide. "Fuck! I left it in my apartment. Did they clean it out yet?"

"I have it," Juan Carlos assured him. "I have some people trying to figure out the manufacturer so we can narrow down who actually bought it."

Joshua exhaled in relief. "Thank you. We've been looking for Teddy for months and nothing but dead ends."

"We'll find him." Juan Carlos pulled out his phone. "Why is Dion calling me? Hey Dion, shouldn't you be on your..." Juan Carlos trailed off. Turning to Aaron, he said, "Turn on the television. Mayor Trainer and Chief Brutus are doing a press conference. The Three Pigs were found dead in their cell, and he released a video of Shadow Guardian and Lobo capturing them."

Aaron rushed out of the room. "That asshole." Mayor Trainer's face illuminated the screen.

"As you see in the video, Detective Aaron Heath did not actually capture the Three Pigs. It was that vigilante and his pet monster that did it." Mayor Trainer said into the microphone. "I, as mayor, do not condone or tolerate vigilante justice. It is reckless and dangerous. I don't doubt that this vigilante justice is what led to the assassination of the Three Pigs in their jail cell."

Mayor Trainer looked straight into the camera. "This is the type of justice you can expect from Felipe Montoya and Detective Aaron Heath. One where suspects don't get their day in court. One where the people take matters into their own hands." Mayor Trainer made his voice grow somber. "The Three Pigs did not deserve to die for simple armed robberies. Their punishment did not fit the crime."

"We need to act." Aaron rushed out into the garden.

CHAPTER 11

GAYMER KEPT CHECKING THE TIME on his phone while he soldered wires to the specialty circuit he designed with the enhanced virtual processor. It was the only thing that could properly read the silicon crystal memory he designed to store the programming of the hypno-box. It was tedious work, but Gaymer loved it.

Needing to take a mental break, Gaymer pushed his goggles back on his head and snatched a pear out of the fruit bowl on his desk. Leaning back in his work chair, he brought up the local news station to see what havoc his uncle caused now that he was trying to be the city hero. Taking a bite of the fruit, Gaymer started the live feed of a press conference that was currently in progress.

"Detective Aaron Heath nor I condone vigilante justice," the young Latinx man on the screen said. "We also don't condone the blatant disregard of our citizens' safety by our police force. While Mayor Trainer and Chief Brutus are so quick to denounce these heroes for their efforts to clean up our streets, we denounce the actions of our local police force and their willful indifference to the Northside." Stepping aside, the man said, "Detective Heath, I believe you have something to add."

A distinguished older man stepped forth, but Gaymer focused on the young man behind him. "Is that Aspen?" Gaymer took another bite, mentally cursing when Detective Heath blocked his view.

"Thank you, Candidate Montoya." He looked into the camera. "Yes, the vigilante known as Shadow Guardian and his associate, Lobo, were the ones that apprehended the Three Pigs. We were alerted by an anonymous source where to find them." An older Latinx man stepped beside him and put a hand on his shoulder. "What happened to the Three Pigs was tragic, but not vigilante justice."

Detective Heath cleared his throat. "I have gathered evidence of the corruption that has plagued our police department, including memos and video evidence. To ensure that this evidence is properly reviewed by Internal Affairs, I have also sent redacted copies to all the local networks. It is time that we clean up this city, and we're going to do that by cleaning up our police force. We will be holding a formal press conference tomorrow. Thank you."

A handsome, muscular Latinx man took Detective Heath's place. "I am Diego Sanz, CEO of DJC. We are committed to the safety of this city and its citizens. That is why we are volunteering the services of our security team while this investigation takes place. They will be taking to the streets and protecting our community once approved by the city council in their emergency meeting tonight. Thank you."

Gaymer tossed the pear core into the trash. He turned his phone off when the video ended. Delighted, he laughed. "Uncle Doug is going to be pissed." Gaymer switched to his text. He read it out loud as he typed.

[You looked cute on camera. Can't wait to game with you tonight.]

Setting his phone aside, Gaymer pulled his goggles back down. "This wire goes here." He closed the casing. "Two done. All that's left is testing them." Gaymer picked up his phone and smiled at the message from Aspen.

[Aspen: I'm going to destroy you tonight.]

[Gaymer: Trash talk. Sexy.]

[Aspen: See you tonight.]

[Gaymer: See you tonight, sexy.]

Gaymer picked up the two tiny earpieces that sat on his desk. He knew they worked. They were the first thing he made before he started working on hypno-boxes. He didn't want his Uncle Doug or that want-to-be-mutt, Brutus, to get any ideas about controlling him.

A tiny robotic golden squirrel with a white underside jumped on Gaymer's desk, causing him to smile. Standing on its hind legs, it cocked its head to the left, then right, like it was studying him with its coal-black eyes. Its metallic furry tail twitched about. It dropped down to all fours.

"What is it, Chitter?" Gaymer set aside the earpieces.

Chitter moved its mouth as if it was talking instead of the tiny voice module in its mouth. "I don't like that you're making these for your uncle. He's a bad man."

"I know, Chitter, but I owe him for raising me and keeping me out of prison when I hacked that bank." Gaymer ran a hand over Chitter's oddly soft metallic fur.

Chitter's tail twitched in agitation. "Who were you hacking that bank for? Huh? You wouldn't have been caught if he hadn't made you do it."

"I shouldn't have told you about that." Gaymer rubbed the top of Chitter's head. "It's not like I can get a job at big bad DJC or anything."

Chitter popped up on its hind legs. "You haven't tried."

"Can we save the lecture for after my game date?" Gaymer asked.

Chitter cocked his head left, then right. "Fine, but we're revisiting this."

"Okay, Chitter." Gaymer rubbed the white metallic fur of its underbelly. "I promise."

CHAPTER 12

"HOW DID HE ORGANIZE THAT press conference so fast?!" Mayor Trainer shouted into the phone. "What type of saboteur are you if you don't know? Remember, you don't get paid unless I win." Mayor Trainer threw his phone across the room.

Brutus caught the phone before it crashed into the wall. "What do we do now?" Mayor Trainer's phone began ringing in his hand. "It's Councilman Cunningham." He tossed the phone back to Mayor Trainer.

"Jasper!" Mayor Trainer said with false excitement. "Sorry." His tone grew grave. "Councilman Cunningham. How can I help you?" He clenched his other hand into a fist. "I understand. We will cooperate fully with the investigation. No, he's right here. We were holding a strategy meeting. I'll tell him. Goodbye."

Catching the flying phone again. "What did that lap dog want?"

"You've been relieved of duty and I've been stripped of power pending the outcome of the investigation." Mayor Trainer spun around, sending an angry fist through the wall. "Those ingrates!"

Moving to his side, Brutus carefully pulled Mayor Trainer's fist from the cracked and broken drywall. "Did you hurt yourself?"

"No." Mayor Trainer opened his hand to let Brutus examine it. "We need to act fast. They want you to turn yourself into custody."

Vehemently, Brutus declared, "I'm not going into a cage."

"I made a promise to protect you at all costs, and I'm going to keep it." Mayor Trainer cradled Brutus's face with his free hand. "No one is putting my baby back in a cage." Brutus let out a soft whimper. "Summon the Puppy Pack. We're going to move our operation to our backup site. You'll go into hiding there."

Brutus growled. "That's where Gaymer is."

"Don't you worry about Gaymer. I've talked to him." Mayor Trainer kissed Brutus hard and passionately. Putting his forehead to Brutus's, he said, "Go now. I'll stall them the best I can."

Brutus hesitantly pulled away. "What about you?"

"I'll be okay," Mayor Trainer reassured him. "Now go. Use the alley exit. We don't want you spotted."

Brutus hesitantly stepped back. "You will come for me, won't you?"

"I'll always come for you," Mayor Trainer said sweetly. Closing his eyes, he took a deep breath before putting authority into his voice. "Go! Now!"

Brutus straightened. "Yes, sir."

Mayor Trainer waited for Brutus to leave before sitting at his desk. Taking a few moments to gather himself, Mayor Trainer flexed the hand he had sent through the wall. Waking his computer, he pressed the button that brought the two external monitors up from the desk.

Mentally preparing himself for the conversation he needed to have, he initiated the call. It took only a moment for the other two to answer. The first to appear was the silhouetted man. On the other screen appeared a young skinny man with mousy brown hair that Mayor Trainer did not recognize.

"I was waiting for your call," the silhouetted man's distorted voice said. "This is Dante's proxy, Finn."

Mayor Trainer couldn't hide the venom in his voice. "This is not something to be handled by underlings."

"Trust me, I am rarely under Dante." Finn gave an impish, toothy grin.

The silhouetted man interjected, "We've seen the press conferences. What is your plan?"

"Brutus is going underground with the Puppy Pack." Mayor Trainer purposely directed his attention toward the silhouetted man. "We are working on a portable hypno-box, one that can be carried by our pups to spread our influence."

Finn laughed. "Is that how you think you're going to win the election?"

"Face it, the election is lost," the silhouetted man spoke in his uncaring tone. "We are going to cut our losses on this venture."

Mayor Trainer slammed his fist on the desk. "You can't do this to me." He narrowed his eyes at the silhouetted man. "And you won't. Remember who alerted you to the Three Bears breaking into the DJC warehouse and whose condo building I let you fill with Dante's mindless pets, the ones that are still there? You owe me more than what you've already given me."

"Dante believes we should see how this plays out, and I agree," Finn announced.

There was a moment of silence before the silhouetted man spoke. "Fine, but under one condition. Gaymer is ours when this is over. Win or lose."

"What do you want with my nephew?" Mayor Trainer asked protectively.

Finn smirked. "Why his skills, of course. The fact that he is eye candy is an added benefit."

"You will not touch him," Mayor Trainer growled through clenched teeth.

"We have a need for his skills," the silhouetted man said calmly. "He will not be harmed."

Mayor Trainer thought for a moment, then reluctantly said, "Agreed, on the conditions that he will not be harmed and he can leave at any time."

"Of course," the silhouetted man responded. "If there's nothing else, we'll adjourn this meeting."

The screens went black. Mayor Trainer picked up his phone and called his nephew. *Gaymer doesn't need to know about this little deal.* Gaymer's voicemail picked up. "Gaymer, we're moving our operations to Fetch Warehouse. Be prepared for company."

CHAPTER 13

"I CAN'T BELIEVE THEY WON'T LET me join the city security force," Joshua griped, slumping back into the couch. "What do they expect me to do all day? I need something to do."

Aiden sat cross-legged beside him. "Um, get your act together? Isn't that what Juan Carlos said?"

"I have my act together," Joshua spat out angrily.

Aiden made a question face at him. "Is it? Because you're acting like a spoiled brat that got told he couldn't have a toy."

"You wouldn't understand what I've been through," Joshua snorted.

Casually, Aiden said, "So tell me."

"Basically, I was kidnapped by the Three Bears and fell in love with one of them. He disappeared after we were rescued." Joshua rolled his eyes. "I went looking for him in the woods, and I can't tell you the rest." Joshua shook his head. "You wouldn't believe me if I did."

Aiden darted his eyes back and forth and pursed his lips. "If I wouldn't believe you, why can't you tell me?"

"Because..." Joshua let out a sound of annoyance. "It's a secret. A big secret. That's why."

Aiden tapped his finger on his cheek in thought. "How about I share an equally big secret?"

"You're not going to let this go, are you?" Joshua sighed. "Fine, but your secret better be pretty big."

Aiden winked at him. "It's not the size of the secret. It's how it can be used against you."

"Yeah, well, fine." Joshua turned so he was facing Aiden. "When I was looking for Teddy, the Bear I developed feelings for, I hurt myself. Jack found me and nursed me back to health. I found out he and Teddy were sort of lovers."

Aiden twisted his face in thought. "So you found out the guy you liked was seeing someone else? Sounds like a Friday night in the bar."

"There's more." Joshua continued, "While Jack was nursing me back to health, we sort of started dating, too."

Aiden grinned widely. "Now this is really sounding like a Friday night in the bars. Are you in a love triangle or a throple?"

"I don't know," Joshua confessed. "When I got there, someone had kidnapped Teddy."

Aiden's eyes grew wide. "Wait, are you serious?"

"Deadly," Joshua answered. "Our only clue was a lipstick called 'Murderous Red.'"

Aiden made a disgusted face. "That sounds tacky, is that the big secret? The guy you liked was seeing someone else, that you're also now seeing and he was kidnapped by someone with bad taste in makeup?"

"No," Joshua groaned. "Well, sort of. Teddy was on Build and Burn."

Aiden snapped his fingers. "When you said 'Bear,' you meant like those dudes that tore up the city. Okay, gotcha."

"Jack was able to purge it from his system because..." Joshua bit his upper lip. Aiden motioned him to go on. "Jack is part Drus."

Aiden cocked his head in thought. "I don't think I know that gay tribe."

"It's not a gay tribe. He's part mystical creature." Joshua waited for Aiden's reaction.

Aiden furrowed his face in thought. "So you're saying he's part mythological creature, and that's the big secret?"

"Yes." Joshua waited for Aiden's ridicule. "After I was better, Jack trained me and we looked for Teddy."

Aiden bounced on the couch. "That is so cool! When can I meet him?!"

"He banished me from the forest when he found a lead on Teddy and didn't want me to come." Joshua was unsure if Aiden believed him or not. "That's why I really want to be on that security force, to see if I can get a lead on Jack or Teddy."

Aiden patted Joshua's knee. "Your secret is safe with me, and Aspen and I will do everything we can to help."

"Thanks, but what can you two do that Juan Carlos and Diego aren't doing already?" Joshua crumpled back onto the couch. "It's hopeless."

Aiden jumped up from the couch. "Hold that thought." He ran down the hall, peeked into Aspen's room, then scurried back. "Okay, he's busy playing his games." Confused, Joshua watched Aiden. "Since you trusted me with your secret. I'm going to trust you with ours." Aiden blurted out excitedly, "Aspen and I are Drag Queens!"

"That's not that big of a secret," Joshua commented. "Juan Carlos is a Drag Queen."

Aiden faltered for a second. He snapped his fingers. "I forgot the super part. We're super Drag Queens."

"What does that mean?" Joshua laughed. "You can lip-sync songs without mouthing peas and carrots?"

Aiden grinned mischievously. "Watch."

Aiden snapped his fingers. A tiny flame appeared between his thumb and forefinger. The flame grew to engulf Aiden's hand, then traveled down his arm. In its wake, it left Aiden's nails long and painted a fiery blend of red and yellow. The flame spread across Aiden's body, leaving him and his clothes transformed rather than burned away.

Stunned, Joshua looked Aiden up and down. He was wearing thigh-high boots, a miniskirt, and a corset. The outfit was all black with twin flames starting at the base of the boots and wrapping around seamlessly to the top of the corset, ending with two explosions on his breast.

The metamorphosis didn't stop there. Aiden's face was painted and contoured perfectly, with hues of red and orange with black cat eyes and sparkling glitter lips. His short blond hair was full and lush, falling down to touch his shoulders.

It started out red and became an umbra into his natural blond.

Aiden twirled on one foot. "Meet Fire."

"Wait," Joshua stared wide-eyed. "Are you mythological, too?"

Fire twirled her hand, creating and extinguishing a fireball. "No, we're not mythological. We're..." she pursed his lips. "We're like special."

"Aspen can do that, too?" Joshua asked in disbelief.

Fire raised both hands and snapped her fingers. Twin flames burned across her, transforming her back to Aiden. He plopped down on the couch. "He's Ice." Aiden nudged Joshua. "Don't tell him I told you."

"I have so many questions," Joshua said in awe. "Like, how?"

Aiden pulled his legs up on the couch. "Well, we think it has something to do with this mysterious rock from outer space our mother examined when she was pregnant with us. It had some strange radiation that we think leaked through her protective clothing and changed us."

"When did you two find out?" Joshua asked, his curiosity getting the better of him.

Aiden laughed. "We were twelve or thirteen." Aiden thought for a second. "No, we were thirteen. We were fighting over something stupid. I think it was a doll or a shirt. I'm not sure what happened, but I remember this explosion that wasn't an explosion between us."

"You turned into teenage Drag Queens?" Joshua asked, a bit bewildered.

Aiden exclaimed, "I wish! We looked like ourselves except I was all fire and red, while Aspen was all ice and blue. When we figured out how to change back, our hair still stayed tipped blue and red. We learned to manipulate our transformations over time, except for our hair. We discovered Drag when we were fifteen and, well, that's all she wrote."

"Wow, do you guys go out and fight crime? Help people in need?" Joshua asked, growing excited.

Aiden let out a sound of derision. "No. I want to, but our parents are worried if they found out about us, we'd be hunted down for research. I think Aspen wants to, but I think he's holding back."

"He is sort of restrained, isn't he?" Joshua commented.

Aiden's tone grew serious. "You don't want to see him when he's not."

"I wish I had some sort of power," Joshua sulked. "Then maybe I could find Teddy or Jack."

Aiden brightened with excitement. "I work for the CEO of DJC. I bet they have a way to give you some sort of power, and I'm going to find it."

CHAPTER 14

ASPEN YAWNED AT HIS DESK. IT WAS one in the morning before he and Gaymer finally finished their online quest. Virtually they battled orcs, trolls, and evil wizards to retrieve the golden chalice that Gaymer presented to him on bended knee. By all rights, it belonged to Gaymer for dealing the death blow, as the squeaky-voiced Chitter, the third in their quest, reminded them.

He couldn't deny that he enjoyed playing with Gaymer. He told off other players that tried to trash-talk Aspen, and those that didn't back down found their characters vanquished. Aspen didn't realize he was doing the same for Gaymer until Chitter complained no one was defending his honor.

"Late night?" Dion asked, walking up.

Aspen stood, trying not to yawn again. "Yes, I had a game date." A rare smile appeared on his stoic features. "I understand you also had a date."

"Yes." Dion smiled playfully. "I will say that Diego did a good job setting me up with Demona."

Aspen tapped on his screen to bring up Dion's calendar. "When should I schedule her in? Do I need to send her an invite to Sunday brunch?"

"We're not at Sunday Brunch yet." Dion laughed. "How long was it before you realized you were obligated to Sunday brunch?"

Impassively, Aspen accused, "You knew that was going to happen, didn't you?"

"Why don't you transfer the calls to Aiden and go grab us some iced coffees?" Dion pulled out her card. "On me as an apology."

Taking the card, Aspen informed her, "You have a marketing meeting in an hour. I've sent you the files and what they are doing wrong."

"You're a superhero." She patted Aspen on the shoulder. "Get us an extra shot. I had a late night, too."

Aiden scoured through the files on his computer. Aspen gave him the basic rundown of how the systems worked. The rest was self-explanatory. He had already updated Diego's calendar with the meetings for the day and updated their shared files with the notes on what the marketing department did wrong with their latest campaign.

He glanced up at the bored security guard stationed here in case of another Code Diego. Feeling bad for the man, Aiden asked, "Do you want something to eat or drink?"

He looked up from his phone. "We're not allowed to eat or drink anything from Diego's personal assistants after the last one drugged the security guard."

"Seriously?" Aiden stood up. He studied the guard. "Do you think you can help me with something?"

Suspiciously he answered, "Depends."

"Can I take your picture?" Aiden pulled out his phone. "You're roughly about the same size as my friend, and I'm trying to design an outfit for him."

Leery of Aiden, he asked, "You don't have a picture of him?"

"We met yesterday, and he's like my new bestie, well, one of my new besties. Have you met Alex? He's Diego's boyfriend. He was the first new bestie I met yesterday. Anyways, Joshua, my second new bestie, needs a pick-me-up. What better way than a new outfit?" Aiden rambled. "So can I? Please?"

The guard put his hands up. "If it will shut you up."

"It won't, but thanks." Aiden came around the desk. "Don't worry, I'm not getting your face." Aiden quickly snapped pictures of the front of the guard. "Now from behind." The guard turned around. "Nice, you don't skip leg day, do you?" Aiden commented, snapping a few more pictures. "Thank you! Do you want to be my new work bestie?"

"No." The guard turned around. "I need to put in for a transfer."

Aiden plopped back into his chair. "Let me know if you change your mind."

"I won't." The guard returned to his position.

Aiden pulled up the picture on his phone, then brought up his editing software. He removed the background, then started making adjustments. He removed the sleeves and tapered the waist. He removed the collar, then added a v-neck. He sketched in a utility belt, then made notes about making the pants tighter.

"Playing a game?" Diego's voice startled Aiden.

Putting his phone done, he stood. "No, working on a side project." He picked up his work tablet. "Now that you're here, you have a busy schedule. You have a marketing meeting in an hour. I sent you notes on their ideas. Basically, they suck. After that, you have an appointment to review Doctor Tyson's updates on his prototype. That takes you through lunch."

"Thank you." Diego smiled happily. "It's so nice not to have to worry about Code Diego's anymore." Diego looked at the bored guard. "I'll tell HR we won't need a guard anymore."

Aiden made his eyes big. "But he's my new work bestie!"

"I'll tell them personally," the guard spoke up. "Have a good day, gentlemen."

Aiden winked at Diego. "He'll come around." Aiden tapped on his tablet. "Hey, I had some questions about this project that was sent back for further development."

"Sure, come into my office." Diego stepped into his office, followed by Aiden. Sitting at his desk, he asked, "What project, and what questions do you have?"

Aiden sat across from him. "There's this project for protective gear that you had Dion test a few weeks ago that had to go back."

"Aww, yes," Diego sighed. "We couldn't maintain the field integrity. Alex is working on a better power source. It basically surrounds the person with this protective electrical field."

Aiden nodded. "Uh-huh. Do you think it could stop a fist or, I don't know, a bullet?"

"Possibly." Diego looked at Aiden questioningly. "It was designed for people who do extreme sports, but our hopes were for security personnel."

Aiden thought for a moment. "What if you didn't protect the whole person? What if you, I don't know, protected just their arms? What would happen if they punched someone or something?"

"It wouldn't amplify their strength, but the field integrity would be stronger and last longer." Diego cautiously asked, "Why?"

Aiden smiled innocently. "No reason." He stood. "When Aspen gets back, do you mind if I ask Alex some questions?"

"Sure," Diego said warily. "Don't take too long. He's still working on a special project for Juan Carlos."

Aiden made a dismissive gesture with his hand. "Ten, maybe fifteen minutes max. I promise." He pointed to the tablet. "Let me know if you have any questions about my notes on the marketing campaign."

"I will, thank you." Diego picked up his tablet and began reading.

Going back to his desk, Aiden pulled out his phone, bringing up the photo editing app. *What if he had gauntlets? Oh, and he'll need a mask! One of those domino ones. Now what could he have for weapons? I'll let him figure that out for himself.*

Gaymer covered his head with his pillow. It did nothing to silence the loud, uninvited, and unwanted guests that showed up while he was gaming with Aspen. Now they were in the warehouse doing whatever his uncle's pet, Brutus, told them. Gaymer was certain they were told to do whatever it took to annoy him.

"Stupid Brutus." Gaymer tossed the pillow off his head and kicked off his sheets. "He better not have touched my stuff." Sitting up and swinging his legs off the bed, Gaymer checked on Chitter lying on his charging pad. Pulling on his cartoon-themed sleep pants and his retro game tee, Gaymer got off his bed.

Gaymer slipped on his shoes, then stepped out of the office-turned-bedroom to the main floor. Thirty or so men were bustling about setting up the isolation chambers, beds and play mats all about. Some of the men wore their Pup hoods, others had theirs attached to their belts. All were men Gaymer wanted out of his sanctuary.

Gaymer's eyes grew wide with anger when he spotted a plump older pup carrying his gaming system out of his workroom. "What the Hell do you think you're doing with that!?" Gaymer yelled, rushing at the pup. "Put that back where you got it right now!"

The plump Pup froze, not knowing what to do with the tiny wild-haired man racing at him. Brutus, dressed in worn denim jeans and a black leather harness, stepped in Gaymer's path. He snatched Gaymer by the collar when he tried to veer around the muscular black man. Gaymer tried to free himself by twisting and turning in his grasp.

"We need something to entertain us," Brutus snarled at the struggling Gaymer.

Slipping out of his shirt, Gaymer skirted around Brutus's swiping hands to snatch his console from the plump Pup. "Then get your own. This is mine."

"You're not going to have time to play it." Brutus took hold of the game console and lifted it with Gaymer dangling from it. "You have work to do."

Gaymer let go of the console and dropped to the floor. "See how much work gets done if you touch my things," Gaymer hissed. "Shall we get Uncle Doug involved?"

"Fine." Brutus shoved the console back into Gaymer's hands. "We need access to the Wi-Fi." Brutus's nose flared in anger. "Make it happen."

Gaymer hugged the console close. "Fine."

"We need real food in this place, too, not that vegetarian crap you got filling the kitchenette," Brutus said, working his jaw in disgust. "Either you make room for it, or I will."

"I'll make room." Gaymer's lips curled into a cruel smile. He really wanted to make a kibble joke, but instead he said, "Anything else, Uncle Brutus?"

"Yes," Brutus snapped. "Keep that robotic rodent away from me and my pups. It creeps us out."

"Yes, Uncle Brutus," Gaymer said with a saccharine smile. "Anything else?"

"No." Brutus's lip twitched with irritation.

"Okay, Uncle Brutus," Gaymer teased, turning and walking away, snatching his shirt off the ground as he made his way back to his workroom.

Joshua stretched on the mat in the building's gym. His tight muscles protested, but Joshua ignored them. He needed to get back into fighting shape. It wasn't because of Aiden's silly plan of turning him into some superhero. He needed to do it in case Jack needed him. He needed to do it for when it came time to rescue Teddy.

Standing, Joshua twisted his body. He felt the release of pressure with the audible crack of his back and the popping of joints. He took several deep breaths to focus his mind. He got into his fighting position. He watched himself in the mirror, mentally critiquing his stance and form as he jabbed and punched the air.

You're dropping your left elbow, he heard Jack say in his head. *Keep your feet planted,* Jack's voice told him. *Protect that pretty face.* Joshua gritted his teeth. He did a combo punch. *You're angry. You'll make mistakes if you fight out of anger.* Joshua threw a punch that sent him off balance, crashing into the mat. *See?*

Joshua rolled onto his back. Closing his eyes, he took a deep, cleansing breath. He pictured the stream that he and Jack went to to train. He heard the gentle babble of the water flowing and felt the cool breeze brush his skin. He could almost smell the scent of the forest. He saw Jack's ruggedly handsome face smiling at him. He missed that face.

Let go of your anger, Jack told him. *We'll find him. I promise.*

Joshua climbed up onto all fours. Opening his eyes, he looked at the uneven bars in the corner of the gym. Jack tried to teach him agility by having him go through obstacle courses he'd configure the forest into. Thankfully, Jack was able to use his abilities to break Joshua's falls, leaving him with only a few bumps and bruises.

I can do this. Joshua shifted into a running stance. *It is not an obstacle. It is simply a difficult path to reach your destination.*

He took off running at full speed. He jumped up into the air, landing and pushing off the lower bar. He grabbed the higher bar. His momentum slung his body swinging up. He turned midair, grabbed the higher bar, then pulled his body up. Getting one foot up on the bar, he pulled himself into a crouching position on the top of the bar.

He sprang from the top of the bar to catch one of the dangling rings from the ceiling. Swinging his body, he reached out and grabbed the other. His arms shook with exertion when he pulled his body into an iron cross. He took a deep breath, exhaling as he dropped down to the floor, landing in a crouch.

I can do this. Joshua wiped the sweat from his brow. *I just have to remember that I'm doing this to protect my men, not avenge them.* Joshua returned to a fighting posture. *Feet planted firmly on the ground.* He punched the air. *Elbow up.* He brought his fist back into a protective stance. *Protect my pretty face.*

CHAPTER 15

THE PARK WAS BUSY WITH PEOPLE enjoying the pleasant weather. Aspen sat on the park bench under the shade of the huge oak tree Gaymer told him to meet him at. The outdoors weren't necessarily Aspen's thing, but he enjoyed the wild unpredictability of nature. It was as soothing as the controlled order of his daily regime.

He smiled, spotting Gaymer with his hair sticking out from a nondescript ball cap, darting through the casually strolling people. He wore a pair of tight jean shorts that he still managed to hang low on his hips to show his anime-themed boxers. Across his white tee, in big bold black lettering, was "Back Off. I Bite." Over his shoulder, he carried a distressed canvas bag decorated with pins and patches.

"I hope you weren't waiting long," Gaymer said, sitting down beside Aspen.

Aspen lied, "Not long at all."

"Park cameras show he's been waiting for approximately seven minutes and forty-three seconds," Chitter's voice came from Gaymer's bag.

Bewildered, Aspen asked, "Did your bag just talk?"

"Chitter!" Gaymer pulled the bag into his lap and opened the flap. "I told you to stay quiet."

Aspen jumped when Chitter popped its head out of the bag. "You also said you'd let me play in the trees."

"Did..." Aspen took a moment to collect his thoughts. "Did that squirrel just talk?"

Gaymer carefully lifted Chitter from the bag. "Yes, and no."

"So this is IceQueen25." Chitter cocked its head curiously at Aspen. "He's cute."

Unnerved, Aspen said, "Thank you."

"Go play, Chitter." Gaymer sat it on the ground. Returning his attention to Aspen, he explained, "I created Chitter when I was twelve." He looked fondly over at Chitter running up a tree. "I was one of those child geniuses that didn't have any friends, so I made one. He made my life not so lonely."

Aspen put a hand on Gaymer's knee. "I can't imagine how hard that was. Growing up, I always had my twin brother, Aiden."

"It's cool." Gaymer pulled out two red-colored water bottles. "As promised. Lunch." He handed a bottle to Aspen. "Dragon fruit tea and veggie and hummus sandwiches." Seeing the confused look on Aspen's face, Gaymer explained, "I'm vegetarian."

Aspen sputtered out nervously. "I'm not. I hope that's okay."

"That depends." Gaymer took a bite of his sandwich.

Unwrapping his sandwich, Aspen asked, "On?"

"How well you kiss," Gaymer said cockily after swallowing down his bite.

Aspen half smirked. "It's going to take more than a picnic in the park for you to find out. I am a lady."

"No, you're a queen." Gaymer pulled out a small bag of chips. Offering it to Aspen, he asked, "Apple chip?"

Alex tapped Diego's foot with his when Dion sat down with them at their table in the rooftop garden of the DJC building. Diego discreetly shook his head no. Alex motioned him to say something, but Diego made a face as he shook his head again. Annoyed, Alex kicked him under the table.

"Ouch!" Diego shouted. "Alex! If you want to know about Dion's date, ask her?"

Amused, Dion looked at Alex. "It went well. No, you are not getting details, and no, she is not coming to Sunday brunch just yet."

"It took us long enough to get you to Sunday brunch," Diego mused.

Alex popped a potato chip into his mouth. "I just wanted to know if it went well and if you are going to see her again."

"It did, and yes, we made plans to see each other again." Dion cracked open her water bottle. "If you must know, we made plans to see each other tonight. I'm going to her bar, In Between."

Diego nearly choked on his burger. "You're—" He cleared his throat. "You're going to In Between."

"Yeah, why?" Dion speared a cucumber in her salad. "Is there a problem?"

Alex coughed. "No, there's no problem at all. It's just that Diego and I were also thinking of going to In Between tonight."

"Oh, that's nice." Dion looked at Alex sternly. "Make other plans."

Smiling tightly, Alex said, "I wanted to stay in, anyways. We'll watch a movie or something." Alex munched on another chip. "I need a mental break from trying to counter that hypnosis thing Juan Carlos has me working on."

"He still has you working on that?" Diego wiped his mouth. "I told you that it was useless without the motherboard I took out of it."

Dion mixed her salad. "You know Juan Carlos."

"He says he's not worried about it, but he asks about it every day," Alex groaned. "I figured out how it works, but I have no clue how to block it or reverse it."

Diego sipped his tea. "Did Aiden come by and ask you about that protective field we tested?"

"Yeah." Alex picked up his burger. "He had some questions that I couldn't answer, so I sent him down to Research and Development to talk to Doctor Tyson."

Dion dropped her fork. "You did what?"

"What?" Alex asked, darting his eyes between the two stunned faces. "Was that not a good idea?"

Dion pulled out her phone. "I'll call HR now."

"Alex, Doctor Tyson is an extreme introvert." Diego shook his head. "I'm not allowed to speak to him directly because he finds me to be too much."

Alex dropped his burger onto the plate. "And I sent your flamboyant personal assistant to go talk to him."

"Yes, send someone now to check on him. I'll hold," Dion said into the phone.

Alex slouched in his chair. "He has so much personality in our emails and instant messages."

"We really need to look into the mental health care of our staff," Diego commented.

Dion made a perplexed face. "Really? Are you sure? Well, okay then. Thank you." Dion hung up the phone. "Apparently Aiden is talking with Doctor Tyson, and they're holding hands."

"So I did good?" Alex asked hopefully.

Diego picked up his burger. "Apparently."

"Now that that catastrophe has been averted," Alex grinned at Dion, "what do you know about Aspen's date? I didn't get a chance to talk to him today."

Dion winked at him. "He's smitten with this Gaymer dude."

Aiden knocked on the door frame. "Doctor Tyson? I'm Aiden, Diego Sanz's new assistant. Do you have a moment?" Aiden eyed the timid young man in an oversized lab coat with thick brown bedhead hair and black-rimmed glasses that turned around. "I was hoping you could answer some questions about the protective field you developed."

"You're not supposed to be here." Doctor Tyson crossed his arms over his chest protectively. "All my interactions are supposed to be electronic."

Aiden inched his way into the lab. "I'll be quick, I promise." He held out his tablet to Doctor Tyson. "I have my questions on this tablet, if you just want to read them. I can be quiet."

"If it'll get you to leave me alone." Doctor Tyson came over and snatched the tablet from Aiden. Turning and walking away, he mumbled to himself, "Hhmm."

Aiden followed him into the lab. "Hhmm, good?" Doctor Tyson glared at him. "Sorry." Aiden made like he was zipping his lips.

"I thought about using multiple protection fields, but we still ran into the problem of keeping them charged. I didn't think about wireless charging." Doctor Tyson turned and nearly collided with Aiden. "Where would they be recharged from? Like a backpack?"

It took Aiden a moment to realize Doctor Tyson wanted him to speak. "No, not a backpack. That would be too bulky. Wait. I have an idea." Aiden pulled out his phone and pulled up the photo he edited before. He showed the picture to

Doctor Tyson. "What about a utility belt? Doesn't DJC make high-capacity batteries?"

"We do." Doctor Tyson took Aiden's phone from him. "What is this? A new guard uniform? It's a bit skimpy and tight."

Aiden quickly lied, "My friend does sexy cosplay. I designed that for him but haven't figured out what material I should use yet."

"Since you helped me..." Doctor Tyson handed the phone and tablet back, then looked at the floor. Nervously, he said, "I'll help you." He then quickly added, "As long as you don't tell anyone."

Aiden crossed his heart with his finger. "Cross my heart."

"We have this stretchy carbon fiber-reinforced polymer fabric that's in the testing phase." Doctor Tyson grabbed his tablet off the table. Timidly he said, "Maybe I could have that costume made for you?"

Aiden hugged Doctor Tyson. "Thank you! That would be awesome!"

"You're touching me," Doctor Tyson said, his body stiff and rigid.

Aiden quickly let go and backed away. "I'm so sorry. I didn't mean to invade your boundaries. Please, forgive me. It won't happen again." Aiden smiled. "Unless you give me permission."

"I, uh, don't know what to do with that information." Doctor Tyson's eyes looked everywhere but at Aiden.

Aiden fought the urge to reach out and touch the uncomfortable doctor. "It means I'm going to respect your boundaries."

"Thank you." Doctor Tyson kept his head down but raised his eyes to look at Aiden. "I guess you can tell I'm not a people person. I prefer to communicate electronically."

Aiden found the doctor oddly endearing. "If you ever get lonely and want company, I'd be happy to come down."

"You're sweet, but I know I probably won't see you after I do this for you." Doctor Tyson lowered his eyes back to the floor. "I'll have the outfit made for you. Thank you for your help with the protection field."

Aiden dropped down into a crouch so he was in Doctor Tyson's line of view. "Hey, I mean it. You seem like a sweet guy. Those are rare." Doctor Tyson shuffled his feet. "I'll come back here every day for my lunch hour and sit quietly until you believe me."

"You can get up," Doctor Tyson said with a slight hint of a smile. "You look silly down there."

Standing up, Aiden said, "If looking silly gets you to believe me, then I'll look silly."

"If I say I believe you, will you still come down and see me?" Doctor Tyson asked shyly.

Aiden blushed. "Of course."

"Good." Doctor Tyson stuck his hands in his lab coat pockets. "I don't feel that weird around you."

Aiden blushed. "Trust me, you're the most normal person in this room."

"I seriously doubt that." Tyson pulled his hands out of his pockets, then jammed them back in.

Bashfully, Aiden asked, "Doctor Tyson, may I shake your hand?"

"Sure." Doctor Tyson hesitantly pulled out a hand and offered it to Aiden. "Call me Tyson, okay?"

Taking his hand, Aiden said, "Thanks, Tyson."

CHAPTER 16

ALEX PLOPPED DOWN ON THE couch in Diego's apartment. He draped his arm over his eyes and groaned. "Diego, can we tell Juan Carlos it's impossible?"

"What is impossible?" Juan Carlos asked, coming out of the kitchen.

Alex popped up quickly. "Juan Carlos, you're here."

"The hypnosis machine," Diego answered for him. "I don't know why you have him working on it, since the machine that was stolen didn't have its motherboard or programming."

Exasperated, Alex said, "Even with Doctor Gingerman's notes, I can't figure out how it works."

"Which means you can't figure out how to stop it or break its control," Juan Carlos finished.

Alex shrugged. "Are you sure we can't talk to Doctor Gingerman?"

"He went on sabbatical a month after that machine was stolen," Diego said, sitting and putting an arm around Alex. "We have no way of contacting him."

Juan Carlos paced. "It has been months since the box was stolen and no one has used it to the best of our knowledge. I guess we can shelve it for now."

"Great." Diego hugged Alex close. "That means Alex can start working on that protection field."

Snuggling close to Diego, Alex said, "I think Doctor Tyson has that covered. He emailed me asking for access to the high-capacity batteries and the wireless charging technology." Alex patted Diego's chest. "He said Aiden gave him the idea."

"Wait." Juan Carlos froze. "Aiden went and saw Doctor Tyson? Who told him he could do that? How bad did Doctor Tyson freak out?"

Diego rubbed Alex's shoulder. "Alex did."

"Apparently it went well," Alex added, smugly. "He and Doctor Tyson have a standing lunch date now."

Juan Carlos sat down across from them. "Really? That is... Wow."

"My thoughts exactly," Diego chuckled. "Aiden is full of surprises."

Alex sighed. "I'm glad you hired him. He brings a little spark to the office."

"He and Aspen did a great job yesterday with the press conference," Juan Carlos commented. "You also did a great job with those drones, Alex."

Diego cocked his head at Juan Carlos. "Didn't you have plans with Aaron tonight?"

"Unfortunately, they had to be canceled." Juan Carlos fell dramatically back into the chair. "Internal Affairs is scrutinizing everyone, especially Aaron. They don't like that we released the redacted information to the press. It's putting a lot of pressure on them to clean up the police force."

Alex shifted off Diego. "Did they find Chief Brutus yet?"

"No," Juan Carlos said solemnly. "He and about thirty other officers have disappeared. It doesn't look good for them.

"At least they stripped Mayor Trainer of power for the time being," Diego commented, with a bit of satisfaction in his voice. "And the DJC City Security has been out in force protecting the streets. I was surprised we had so many people volunteer for it."

Alex patted Diego's leg. "It's their city, too, and they were tired of the corruption and crime."

"Shadow Guardian may see retirement in his future," Diego said wistfully.

Juan Carlos pulled out his small black disc. "That reminds me, I meant to ask you about this yesterday, but with everything going on, I forgot."

"Is there something wrong with it?" Diego leaned forward to take the disc.

Juan Carlos mulled his answer over. "Yes, and no."

"Can we not be vague? My brain is fried." Alex plucked the disc from Diego's hand. "I can run a diagnostic, but I need to know what I'm looking for."

Juan Carlos waved his hand dismissively. "It could be nothing. I might be making a big deal about nothing."

"Juan Carlos," Alex whined. "Brain fried, remember?"

Diego gave Juan Carlos an imploring look. "Please, don't break my boyfriend."

"Fine, well, when I used that disc to open Joshua's door," Juan Carlos explained. "It unlocked the two door locks like it was supposed to, but then it did something I didn't tell it to do."

Interested, Diego leaned forward. "What?"

"It slipped behind the door and opened the door latch that would have stopped me from opening the door, but that wasn't the strange part." Juan Carlos paused in thought.

Leaning forward beside Diego, Alex said, "Go on, now you've got my interest. It shouldn't have done that without instruction."

"I know. It's what it did when I complimented it on doing a good job that was unexpected." Juan Carlos leaned forward and spoke in a hushed tone. "It smiled at me." Diego burst into laughter. Annoyed, Juan Carlos leaned back in his chair. "I should have known you must have programmed it to do that as some kind of joke."

Puzzled, Diego said, "I didn't do anything. I thought you were joking."

"You're serious? It shouldn't respond to anyone's voice, unless..." Alex paused, holding up the disc to look at it closer. "Whoops."

Diego turned his head to Alex. "What do you mean, 'whoops?'"

"Yes, what do you mean, 'whoops?'" Juan Carlos asked suspiciously.

Feeling their scrutiny, Alex shrank back into his seat. "After our encounter with that demon twink—"

"Are we still calling him that?" Diego interrupted.

"Yes." Juan Carlos motioned Alex to continue. "Go on."

Guiltily, Alex continued, "I've been working on the AI of the microbots, trying to get it to anticipate Diego's actions and operate independently in case he gets incapacitated."

"What did you do?" Diego asked suspiciously.

Alex cringed. "I may have given it basic intelligence with the ability to adapt and learn. I must have gotten this disc from that batch instead of your normal suit."

"Explain it to me like I'm the man that's going to yell at you for what you did," Juan Carlos demanded in his fatherly tone.

Shaking his head, Diego closed his eyes. "He brought the suit to life."

"Well, not the suit, exactly," Alex corrected. "I didn't want to risk the life of my handsome and sexy boyfriend that I'm finally going to let take me on an extravagant vacation."

Diego opened one eye to look at Alex. "What did you do?"

"It was just the microbot disc I gave Juan Carlos." Alex smiled guiltily. "I got it from a batch of microbots I've been working on in private."

Diego looked at Juan Carlos. "Do you want to or shall I?" Juan Carlos motioned for Diego to continue. "What were you thinking?"

"That by using a separate group of microbots, I wouldn't be risking your life." Alex smiled innocently. "So, where are we going on vacation?"

Juan Carlos laughed. "Oh, he's good."

"Not that good." Diego eyed Alex suspiciously. "What else did you do?"

Alex bit his lower lip. The guilt was written all over his face. "In order to test it, I've had to wear the suit. Well, part of it."

"You tried it on?!" Juan Carlos's disapproval was obvious. "I thought you would know better."

Alex winced. "It's only large enough to cover my upper body. I took all the safety precautions."

"He's not telling us something," Diego observed. "Out with it."

Alex smiled big. "Don't you want to talk about the vacation instead?"

"Aye, dios mio." Juan Carlos shook his head. "Alex, what is it?"

Shrinking back, Alex admitted, "It sort of bonded with me. It reacts whenever it sort of sees me." Alex braced himself for the scolding. "I've been setting it in its container beside me while you're on patrol, so it doesn't get lonely and we sort of play games together."

"He turned it into a pet." Diego shook his head in disbelief.

Juan Carlos looked from Diego to Alex. "Will someone explain to me exactly why I am mad at Alex?"

"He basically created a sentient set of microbots that can act independently," Diego explained.

"That's the one line I wasn't ready to cross. We have strict policies and procedures about it at DJC."

Alex tried to make his voice sound as innocent as possible. "I don't work for DJC. I work for JCA Research, remember?"

"He's got you there." Juan Carlos laughed.

Diego glared at Juan Carlos. "You're not helping any."

"Alex, perhaps you should show it to us." Juan Carlos stood. "Then you and Diego can plan your vacation together."

In the secret command base, Alex stood at his workstation nervously looking at a curious Juan Carlos and a frowning Diego looking toward his little corner. "Please, don't scare it."

"We won't scare it," Juan Carlos reassured him before popping Diego in the head. "Quit scowling. You'll get wrinkles."

Diego rubbed the back of his head. "What was that for?"

"I told you, to keep from getting wrinkles," Juan Carlos answered. "Also, because you're brooding is making Alex nervous."

Diego closed his eyes and exhaled his anger. Smiling, he opened his eyes. "Okay, I'm ready. Show us."

"Keep an open mind." Alex slid open the panel on the wall and pulled out a glass box with microbots moving about in it. Alex sat it on the desk. "It's okay, they know. You can show yourself."

Juan Carlos and Diego shared a look when the microbots did nothing. "Are you sure you gave it intelligence?" Diego asked.

"Diego," Juan Carlos chided. "Be nice."

Alex pulled out the disc from Juan Carlos and held it over the box. "I told you, they know." A tentacle of microbots tentatively reached up, then snatched the disc from Alex's hand. "Come on, don't be shy. They want to meet you."

The microbots swirled together to form a generic face. It looked at Diego, then Juan Carlos. It shot a tentacle out to Alex's left arm and swirled itself up Alex's shirt sleeve. A small portion of it poked its head out, then pulled itself out to wrap around Alex's waist and chest with the tentacle head peeking up over Alex's shoulder.

"He's scared," Alex explained. "It's okay. They're friends. That's Diego, the one I help as Shadow Guardian." The tentacle looked at Alex, then at Diego. It made a simple smiley face at him. "He likes you."

Juan Carlos stepped around the desk. "Amazing." He reached out a hand to touch it, but it recoiled away. "Did I do something wrong?"

"No." Alex ran a hand to stroke the microbots. "It really doesn't know you."

Diego came around the other side and stuck out his hand. The microbots snaked around his arm and then around his body. "Why does it like me and not Juan Carlos?"

"It likes Shadow Guardian and you're Shadow Guardian," Alex explained simply. "It actually helps me sometimes when I'm running multiple screens."

Juan Carlos stepped closer, careful not to startle the microbots. "Why do you keep calling it an 'it?' Doesn't it have a name?"

"Not yet." Alex ran a hand over the snaking tendril. "I didn't think to give it a name."

Diego brought the end of the tendril to his face. "Do you want a name?" The tendril motion up and down. "What would you like to be called?"

"It doesn't talk," Alex explained.

Juan Carlos scoffed. "It's obviously smart. Look what it did for me at Joshua's house. I'm sure it can communicate in some way." The tendril turned to Juan Carlos. It twisted like a person, turning its head with recognition. It shot off of

Diego to wrap around Juan Carlos. "What's it doing? Attacking?!" Juan Carlos asked in a panic.

"I think the disc's memory just finished integrating." Alex laughed as the tendril rested on Juan Carlos's shoulder. "It remembers you."

Juan Carlos stroked the tendril. "Well, I'm glad. I can't have a grandchild of mine being terrified of me."

"Grandchild?" Alex and Diego blurted simultaneously.

"Yes, it is technically a child you two made together." Juan Carlos made kissing sounds to the tendril's smiling face. "Diego's microbots and Alex's programming." The tendril rippled, taking in the new information. It uncurled from Juan Carlos and slithered across the floor. "What's it doing?"

Alex moved to follow it. "I don't know."

"It's heading to the Shadow Guardian control panel!" Diego said in a panic, rushing to follow Alex.

Calmly, Juan Carlos strolled over. "You're overreacting. Let's see what it does. If it wanted to harm us, it could have easily done so earlier."

The tendril formed a hand on the end and began tapping buttons. A keyboard appeared on the screen. The tendril typed quickly. Over the speakers came, "Are you my family?"

"See." Juan Carlos smiled proudly. "Yes, we are your family. Diego and Alex are your fathers, and I am your abuela."

The tendril typed again. "Alex is my father. Diego is my father. Juan Carlos is my abuela."

"You couldn't be abuelo, could you?" Diego teased.

Juan Carlos glared at Diego. "Hush, don't confuse your son, err, daughter, um, non-binary child?"

"Amazing." Alex took a seat at the console and watched the tendril. "What do you want us to call you?"

The tendril reformed. It looked at Alex, then at Diego. It moved between the two for some moments, as if in thought, before forming a hand and typing again. "*A l* from Alex and *g o* from Diego. Algo."

Juan Carlos made a face. "May I suggest, Alegro? *A l* for Alex, *e g* for Diego, and *r o* for robotic. That way, its name is happy instead of something."

The tendril made a huge smiling face, then turned into a hand. "I like that. Call me Alegro, because I am happy. I am happy to have all of you."

"I like that, too." Diego stuck out his chest proudly. He put a hand on Alex's chest.

Alex beamed at Alegro. "I can't believe we accidentally created a child together."

"Well, I guess you two have a lot to talk about." Juan Carlos reached out to let Alegro wrap around him. "Now that you have a kid together, Alex has to move in, and what are you going to do about daycare while the two of you are at work? I won't have my grandbaby sitting alone all day in a bowl."

Stunned, Alex said, "Wait, who said I was moving in?"

"Who are we going to get to babysit it?" Diego blurted out.

Juan Carlos pointed at Alex with his other hand. "I said you're moving in. It's time. You two love each other, and you practically live together already." He pointed to Diego. "Not my problem, but I may know someone. In the meantime, Alex can take Alegro to work with him. His office is private." Smiling at Alegro, Juan Carlos added sweetly, "Now, if you two don't mind, I'd like to show my grandbaby the garden."

"We're parents," Alex said in disbelief.

Diego patted his shoulder. "And you agreed to move in and let me take you on a vacation." Alex looked up at a grinning Diego. "Don't worry, I'll let you be the one that proposes."

Alex's face went white.

CHAPTER 17

MAYOR TRAINER LOOKED DOWN from his office window at the media circus that perched on his doorstep. *Fucking vultures!* He turned his attention to the DJC security personnel that stood guard at his door. *Damn Diego Sanz and Juan Carlos Sanz. If it weren't for them, Brutus would be here at my side.*

"Mayor Trainer, sir." Keagan, Mayor Trainer's timid assistant, appeared in the doorway. He cringed when Mayor Trainer turned to face him. "I, uh, sent out the statement that you have no comment on the ongoing investigation and that you are not currently aware of Chief Brutus's location." His voice cracking, Keagan asked, "You don't know where he is? Do you?"

Mayor Trainer's nostrils flared with anger. "Of course I don't! How dare you even ask me that?!"

"I'm sorry, sir." Keagan cringed. "I shouldn't have asked."

Mayor Trainer stormed across the room to his desk. "Have the arrangements been made for me to attend the debate tomorrow?"

"Yes, sir, sort of." Keagan cautiously stepped to the desk. "Due to the circumstances, they have asked that your presence be virtual."

Sitting down, Mayor Trainer nodded. "Understandable. Have you made the arrangements yet?"

"Y-yes, s-sir," Keagan stuttered out. "I, uh, thought it best for you to do it in here. If you don't mind, that is, sir."

Mayor Trainer turned to look at the fist size hole in his wall. "I'll need something to cover that."

"Y-yes, sir. I'll get right on that," Keagan stammered, his eyes darting left and right.

Turning back to face Keagan, Mayor Trainer rolled his eyes at his trembling assistant. "I can assure you that Brutus is not here or in my home." Keagan visibly relaxed. "You need to get over this irrational fear of him. He is my fiancé."

"Oh, wow. Congratulations," Keagan responded, not knowing what else to say. "Do I need to draft a statement?"

Mayor Trainer slammed his fist down on the desk, causing Keagan to jump back. "Of course not, you fool! There will be no announcement until this Internal Affairs witch hunt is over, and we've been sworn back into office."

"Apologies. I don't know what I was thinking." Keagan glanced at the door. "If there isn't anything else..."

Mayor Trainer waved him off. "Go. I have no further use for you."

"Good night, sir." Keagan bowed his head. "I will see you tomorrow." He took a step back, then said, "Congratulations, again," before scurrying out of the office.

Mayor Trainer waited for the sound signaling Keagan set the alarm before initiating the video call. Gaymer's annoyed expression filled the screen. "Gaymer, how is your progress going?"

"Hello, Uncle. I'm well, a little annoyed to have my space invaded by your stupid mutts," Gaymer quipped irritably.

Mayor Trainer spoke diplomatically through clenched teeth and a fake smile. "I know it's a minor inconvenience. We all must make sacrifices for the greater good."

"They touched my things." Gaymer's anger didn't hide the hurt in his voice. "I went to the bathroom and came back to find two of those mongrels chasing Chitter around my lab!"

Chitter popped up onto Gaymer's lap and did its best to hug him. "It's okay, Gaymer. They didn't hurt me."

"I know." Gaymer snuggled the robotic squirrel. Fury was in his watery eyes when he turned them on his uncle. "I'm tired of hearing how much I owe you, Uncle Doug. You owe me for hacking all those financial institutions for you! For hiding your black market dealings and all the rest!" With one hand, he held Chitter close to his chest. The other he tapped on the screen to bring up a small window pop-up in the lower right. "This is an encrypted cloud drive with every scandalous detail and dark secret about your life." The window disappeared. "If Chitter doesn't send a reset code, it decrypts and releases." He put his arm back around Chitter. "Are we clear, Uncle Doug?"

Despite his anger, Mayor Trainer could not fault his nephew for doing what he needed to protect Chitter. He'd do the same for Brutus. He was doing that now for Brutus. It was a family trait. One that brought Gaymer to his doorstep when his sister dove off the ocean liner to rescue her husband.

"Crystal." Mayor Trainer's voice was uncharacteristically soft and fatherly. "I will reiterate to Brutus how important you and Chitter are to me. I will also have him paint a ten-foot boundary between your area and theirs that no Pup is allowed to cross. Okay?"

Gaymer wiped away a tear. "Even Brutus?"

"Even Brutus," Mayor Trainer said with a reassuring smile. "Now, may I have an update?"

Gaymer took a moment to nuzzle Chitter before answering. "I was able to make a one-hand device." Gaymer set Chitter aside and picked up the black leather glove. "I was able to use the specialty circuit fabric I created to keep it from being bulky. It is activated by splaying your fingers out."

"Nice. How long will it take to make more?" Mayor Trainer asked sweetly.

Gaymer set the glove aside. "This is just the prototype. The only reason I was able to get this one done so fast was because I had a spool of the circuit fabric on hand. It takes three days for the printer to spin another full spool." Gaymer picked up one of the tiny earpieces. "I have three pairs of these neutralizers, but I can't make any more if I'm printing more fabric. I can do one or the other."

"Focus on the fabric." Mayor Trainer strummed his fingers on the desk. "In the meantime, my Pups will need some items to help them disrupt the city to ensure my victory."

Fervently, Gaymer said, "I do not make deadly weapons."

"Fine. Then make them non-deadly, but I need them by morning," Mayor Trainer conceded. "Now, I will have a word with your Uncle Brutus."

Gaymer gave a saccharine sweet smile. "Good night, Uncle."

Mayor Trainer waited a moment after Gaymer's video ended before calling Brutus. He couldn't help but smile when he saw the handsome black man appear on his screen. "Brutus," he said sweetly. "I miss you. Are you settling in okay?"

Brutus gave him a rare smile. "We are settling in, though Gaymer has not made it easy."

"Yes, about Gaymer." Mayor Trainer strummed his fingers on the desk. "I want you to keep the Pups away from Chitter. If anything happens to that robotic squirrel, you and the Pups involved will answer to me."

Brutus's smile faded to a frown. "Yes, sir."

"I also want a line marking ten feet from his workspaces. No Pup, including yourself, is to cross that line." Mayor Trainer's voice grew stern. "Is that understood?"

Brutus grumbled, "But sir—"

"Are you disobeying me?" Mayor Trainer scolded. "I know you're not being a bad Pup and disobeying me."

Brutus shook his head. "No, sir."

"Good." Mayor Trainer smiled sweetly at him. "Without Chitter, Gaymer is useless to me and all of our plans are ruined.

Brutus nodded. "I understand, sir. Your orders shall be carried out."

"Good." Mayor Trainer smiled wickedly. "I have Gaymer working on weapons for the Pups. Tomorrow our Puppy Patrol shall begin wreaking havoc on our fair city."

CHAPTER 18

"HONEY! WE'RE HOME!" AIDEN cried out as he and Aspen entered the apartment. "Do you have our three olive martinis ready?"

Joshua stepped out of the kitchen wearing an apron and a questioning look. "Three olive martinis?"

"We watched a lot of old shows when we were younger," Aspen explained. "We don't drink, anyways."

Aiden sniffed the air. "What are you cooking?"

"I hope you two are hungry." Joshua grinned proudly. "I made lemon pepper chicken with boxed stuffing, steamed green beans, and a salad."

"We can cook for ourselves. You don't have to cook for us." Aspen took a deep whiff of the delicious smell coming from the kitchen. "But, you did go to all the trouble and it would be rude not to at least try it."

Bashful, Joshua said, "It was no trouble at all, and it's sort of a thank you for being so cool with this situation." Joshua smirked. "Plus, I wanted to hear about your lunch date with Gaymer."

Aiden groaned, shoulder-bumping his brother. "He won't even tell me about it, and I'm his brother."

"Look who's talking." Aspen returned the gesture. "I had to hear about you and Doctor Tyson from Dion."

Joshua cut in. "You two go get changed for dinner. I want to hear about both of your dates." Returning to the kitchen, Joshua announced, "By the way! You two are doing the dishes!"

After dinner, with the dishes done and the meager leftovers put away, Joshua sat with Aiden on the couch while Aspen went to prepare for his gaming date with Gaymer. Aiden sat with his feet in Joshua's lap, reading a book, while Joshua flipped through the channels, trying to find something to watch.

Putting his book down, Aiden said, "You know I have plenty of books you can read if you don't like what's on television."

"I'm just restless." Joshua turned off the television. "I was training for most of the day down in the gym,"

Pulling his feet under him, Aiden asked, "That explains why you were so hungry. I'm surprised we had any leftovers."

"It was weird," Joshua commented. "I had the entire gym to myself the entire day. I kept expecting someone to come in, but no one ever did."

Setting his book aside, Aiden explained, "Alex told me we get access to the private gym, the one that Diego uses and he pretends to use."

"That would explain it," Joshua said, relieved. "I thought people were avoiding me."

Aiden's eyes grew big with excitement. "I almost forgot!" He pulled out his phone. "I designed you a costume and Tyson is making it for you!" He handed the phone to Joshua. "It's sexy and sassy."

"You want me to wear this?" Joshua looked at the phone, then at Aiden. "It's a little..." Joshua fumbled for the right word, "tight, isn't it?"

Casually, Aiden said, "Tyson is using this special fabric that conforms to your body and acts like body armor."

"I don't have any superpowers, though." Joshua handed him back the phone. "I can fight and I can jump around, but I can't do what you do."

With a mischievous grin, Aiden checked the hallway for Aspen. He swiped the screen on his phone. "You will with these." He handed the phone back. "They are like protection fields. I sort of put the idea in Tyson's head to make gauntlets. You'll be able to block blasts and hit things without harming yourself."

"Cool, but why is he making these for you?" Joshua asked, studying the picture.

"Well..." Joshua didn't like the guilty tone of Aiden's voice. "He thinks he's making them for Diego."

Joshua handed the phone back. "No."

"He's making two sets," Aiden said, taking the phone back. "Diego will get one set and you'll get the other."

"No," Joshua repeated.

Aiden jumped up off the couch. "We can test it for him." He grabbed Joshua by the arm. "Come on, let's go downstairs and you can show me your skills."

"Alright, but leave a note for Aspen, so he doesn't worry." Joshua begrudgingly stood up. "Let me get changed."

"Okay," Joshua said, stretching. "I'm going to run to those uneven bars, do some tricks, then grab the rings, then land."

Aiden snapped his fingers, igniting a small flame that spread across his body, turning him into the explosive Fire. "Let's see you do it while dodging my fireballs."

"Wait a minute now." Joshua took a step back. Fire formed a fireball and tossed it at Joshua's feet. "Hey!"

Fire formed another fireball. "Don't worry. They won't burn you. I control them." She tossed the fireball up in her hand. "Now run!" She hurled the fireball at Joshua.

Joshua took off running toward the uneven bars. He heard the sizzle of fire coming from behind him. He chanced a look to see one of Fire's fireballs coming at him. He parried, letting it scorch by. He heard the crackle of flame from two more of Fire's blasts. He dodged one, then jumped up into the air to miss the other, grabbing the lower bar and spinning himself to perch on the top.

"Now, hold on one—" Joshua started before leaping backward to dodge another blast. He grabbed the higher bar and spun around twice, then perched on the top. "Will you—" Joshua propelled himself off the bar just as a fireball flew under his feet. Catching one of the rings he gasped, "Oh shit!" He let go of the ring right as a fireball struck the ring.

Joshua braced for the hard impact of the ground. Instead, a second later his butt hit something hard and cold, and he began sliding down an ice slide that carried him across the room back to Fire and the disapproving glare of Aspen, whose hand wore a white glove that stopped at his wrist.

"Do you two have something you'd like to tell me?" Aspen asked. A small blue ball appeared on the tip of his finger that traveled along the glove, returning his hand to normal. "Who would like to go first? Joshua?" He turned his cold stare on his brother. "Or you Fire?"

Fire reached down and pulled Joshua up. "We were training and I guess I got a little carried away."

"We need a safe word for next time." Joshua brushed the ice from his shorts.

Aspen looked at them with disbelief. "Next time? You shouldn't have done it this time!"

"It's okay, Aspen." Fire moved to stand beside Joshua. "He's going to be a superhero."

Steam hissed from where Aspen poked Fire in the chest. "He's going to end up dead, and who gave you permission to tell him our secret?"

"He told me after I told him my secret." Joshua stepped in. "He's helping me train so I can find my boyfriends. Teddy and Jack."

Aspen's hair went white as ice. "Juan Carlos told us that you weren't supposed to be going out looking for them."

"So you knew one of his boyfriends is a Drus and the other was one of the Three Bears that destroyed Northside and didn't tell me?" Fire crossed her arms. Sparks popped around her as she began to glow. "I thought we told each other everything."

The blue ball returned to the tip of Aspen's finger and rapidly traveled across the young man's body transforming his business casual attire to fitted blue chest armor that cut sharply down to her groin, giving the illusion of a blue heart with swirls of white around her breasts that joined in the middle of her bosom to continue down her body in a zig-zagged line.

The short skirt she wore was made of long shards of pointed white icicles that matched her snow-white, fingerless, wrist-length gloves. Her six-inch clear stilettos gave her added height, as did the high ponytail with a swoop that allowed her blue and white streaked hair to cascade down around her shoulders.

"I don't know what you're talking about," Ice said with cold anger, the water in the air freezing and misting with her breath. "What I know is you shared our secret without asking me, and now you're down here training in secret to be some kind of superhero."

Joshua moved between the two. He felt the heat of Fire on one side, and the cold of Ice on the other. "Guys, err, girls, please, can we talk calmly?"

"That's all she wants to do," Fire shot out. "Talk. Never take any action."

Snow began to fall in the gym. "All she wants to do is jump in head-first. She never thinks about the consequences."

"Stop it, both of you!" Joshua shouted. "I feel like I'm getting freezer burned between the two of you."

Fire and Ice took a step back. They nodded to each other, then transformed back into Aspen and Aiden. "I'm sorry," Aspen said, running a hand through his hair. "Our parents don't want us revealing our abilities in case some government agency decides to try to weaponize us."

"I trust Joshua, don't you? He shared with me about his boyfriends, and I figured it would be okay to share our secret with him." Aiden took Aspen's hand. "I should have asked you first."

"I should have trusted you to know who to share our secret with and who not to." Aspen pulled his brother into a hug. "Promise me you two aren't going out on the town as superheroes."

Joshua cleared his throat. "That was me, and I wasn't going out as some superhero. I was training to make sure I could help Jack and Teddy in case they needed me."

"I promise!" Aiden vibrated with excitement in Aspen's arms. "I designed a costume for him! Want to see?!"

CHAPTER 19

ALEX PUSHED THE VEGETABLES around his plate. "I can't believe we couldn't find a single trace of Chief Brutus last night."

"Alex," Diego said sternly. "Quit playing with your food and eat your vegetables."

Setting his fork down, Alex said, "I'm not playing with my food. I don't like zucchini."

"How can we expect our child to eat their vegetables if you won't?" Diego scolded, finishing the last of his zucchini spears.

Alex rolled his eyes. "Alegro doesn't eat."

"It's the principle." Diego tapped Alex's plate. "Set a good example for our child and eat your vegetables."

"You should eat your vegetables." Dion took the empty seat at the lunch table. "You don't want Chef Sven coming out here and yelling at you for wasting food." She speared a zucchini spear. "The only thing that matches the wrath of Juan Carlos is being yelled at by a Swedish chef—in Swedish."

Alex stabbed a zucchini spear with his fork. "Fine."

"So, when did you two have a child?" Dion's casual question almost caused Alex to choke on his bite.

Diego cleared his throat uncomfortably. "Um, we don't." He patted Alex on the back. "We were, um, what were we doing, Alex?"

"I decided to move in with Diego last night." Alex gulped down some water. "He's being," Alex cut his eyes at Diego, "Diego."

Dion popped another zucchini spear into her mouth. "Makes sense."

"Yeah, it does," Diego said with relief. "Hey! Wait! What does that mean?"

Alex popped a zucchini spear into Diego's mouth. "It means you have two settings. Over the top and business serious."

"Since this isn't business..." Dion smirked.

Swallowing the zucchini down, Diego grumbled, "There's more to me than that."

"There's a lot more to you than that." Dion patted his hand. "Now, congratulations on you two finally moving in together."

Diego beamed. "Thank you. I don't know why it took so long. He practically lives there as it is."

"Diego," Alex warned. "Don't start."

Dion laughed softly. "You two. I can't wait for the wedding."

"No." Alex covered Diego's mouth with his hand. "You said I get to be the one that proposes."

Diego moved Alex's hand from his mouth. "I wasn't going to say anything other than I prefer a spring wedding, in Juan Carlos's garden, when the flowers are blooming."

"Change of subject," Alex said, exasperated. "How are you and Demona doing?"

A coy smile crossed Dion's lips. "We're going well. She is so fascinating."

"And it was all because of me." Diego puffed out his chest proudly.

Relenting, Dion said, "Yes, because of you. Now, I need some gossip. How are Aiden and Doctor Tyson doing?"

"I'll trade you Aiden and Doctor Tyson gossip for Aspen and Gaymer gossip." Alex snuck a zucchini spear onto Diego's plate.

Dion smiled broadly. "Deal. Okay, so they were up until eleven playing their online games. I caught him texting Gaymer today when he was supposed to be working on a report for me..." Dion paused for dramatic effect. "And he was smiling."

Alex and Diego dramatically gasped. "Can you imagine? Strict and stoic Aspen, not only goofing off, but smiling?"

"Maybe he'll be nicer to me," Diego mused.

Alex leaned over and pecked Diego on the cheek, covertly moving the rest of his zucchini to Diego's plate. "Probably not."

"Aww, thank you." Diego switched their plates. "Now eat your vegetables or no dessert for you."

Alex reluctantly ate another zucchini spear. "Meanie."

"Anyways, he's having lunch with Gaymer right now," Dion said conspiratorially. "I'll have more for you later. Now Aiden and Doctor Tyson."

Alex swallowed down the last of his zucchini. "I hate zucchini."

"Don't worry, we're having squash for dinner." Diego smiled impishly.

Alex rolled his eyes. "Anyways, Aiden and Doctor Tyson have been instant messaging all day."

"I didn't think that boy could smile any bigger," Diego added. "He has a glow about him."

Alex leaned forward. "Doctor Tyson actually sent me a message saying Aiden helped him come up with a solution for his shield prototype."

"Wait." Dion held up a finger. "He actually messaged you?"

Smugly, Alex leaned back in his chair and crossed his arms. "He not only messaged me about the prototype, he also asked me if I knew anything about Aiden."

"He's been casually asking me about Doctor Tyson all morning." Diego smirked. "Every time I came by his desk, he'd hide his messaging program and pretend he was working on something else."

Dion mused. "Our boys have it bad."

"Yeah, Aiden nearly knocked me over on his way to Doctor Tyson's office." Alex laughed. He pulled out his phone. "Hey, what's this alert?"

Diego pulled out his phone. "I got one, too. There's some sort of robbery in progress."

"Oh, dear." Dion covered her mouth. "It's at Tuli's. That's where Aspen went with Gaymer."

Diego nodded to Alex before turning to Dion. "Contact the head of city security. See what you can find out. Alex and I will see if Aaron knows anything."

"Right." Dion stood. "Let me know if you find anything out."

Alex waited for Dion to leave before saying, "Shadow Guardian?"

"Shadow Guardian," Diego confirmed.

Getting up, Alex put his phone to his ear. "I better call Aiden. Damn, voicemail. Aiden, there's a robbery at the restaurant Aspen is at. Call me when you get this." Alex put his phone away.

"We'll get word to him." Diego stood.

Nervously, Alex said, "You've never gone out with this much light out."

Diego thrust his shoulders back and puffed his chest out. "We can do this." He took Alex by the hand. With more confidence than he felt, he said, "It's time to bring the shadow to the light."

Aiden took a deep breath to calm himself before stepping into the lab. "Doctor Tyson, I'm here for our lunch date," he said, merrily strolling in as if his stomach wasn't tied in knots.

"Aiden." There was a hint of surprise and joy in Doctor Tyson's voice when he looked up and saw the young man enter. "I have that costume for you. Do you want to see?"

Trying not to sound too excited, Aiden said, "Sure." He sat on an empty stool at Doctor Tyson's workstation. "What about your prototype? I didn't keep you from working on that, did I?"

"Oh, no." Doctor Tyson pulled out a folded shiny black and gold set of clothes. "I hope your boyfriend likes it."

Aiden held up the sleeveless shirt. "Boyfriend?" He laughed. "He's not my boyfriend. He's my roommate. He has a boyfriend." Aiden then corrected himself. "He has two boyfriends, in fact."

"Wow. I've never had one." Hopeful, Doctor Tyson asked, "Do you like it?"

Aiden folded the shirt back up. "I love it. Thank you." Shyly, Aiden asked, "May I hug you? I really want to hug you."

"I guess." Doctor Tyson blushed.

Aiden jumped up from the stool and hugged a shocked Doctor Tyson tightly. "You are amazing! Thank you! Thank you! Thank you!"

"You're... you're welcome." Doctor Tyson tentatively put his arms around Aiden and tapped him on the back before pulling back. "It was nothing, really."

Sitting back down and pushing the outfit aside, Aiden asked, "How is your prototype going? Did you finish it?"

"I did. I made two sets. I was hoping you'd take them to Mr. Sanz for me. He overwhelms me sometimes." Doctor Tyson pulled out a small box. "I hope you don't mind, but I used the designs from your costume." He held up a gauntlet and a black utility belt. "They just seemed to work with the idea you gave me yesterday."

"Of course, I'll take them to Diego for you!" Aiden took the gauntlet from Doctor Tyson. "I can't believe you used my designs! These look fantastic!"

"You don't mind?" Doctor Tyson asked shyly, pushing his glasses back up. "If you do, I can find some other—"

Aiden cut him off. "Don't you dare!"

"Okay." Doctor Tyson took a step back.

Aiden set the gauntlet down. "I'm sorry. I didn't mean to yell. I can be a bit, um, extra sometimes."

"It shows you have passion." Doctor Tyson started rubbing his hands together. "Now that you have your costume, I'm guessing you won't be coming back to see me."

Aiden took Doctor Tyson's hands in his. "Why wouldn't I come back? You are fascinating."

"No, I'm not." Doctor Tyson turned his head away from Aiden. "I'm a crazy scientist that doesn't like being around people. You, you're like a blazing sun, lighting up the darkness with your beauty."

Aiden's heart thumped harder in his chest. "That was the sweetest thing anyone has ever said to me." He got off the stool so he was standing face to face with Doctor Tyson. "May I kiss you?"

"You can, but I know you really don't want to." Doctor Tyson turned his face away from Aiden.

Aiden gently cradled Doctor Tyson's chin. "Yes, I really do." He turned Doctor Tyson's face to look at him. "I really do." Aiden pressed his lips to Doctor Tyson's. He ignored the buzz of the phone in his pocket. Doctor Tyson put his arms around Aiden. They deepened the kiss.

Aiden's phone began buzzing again in time with Doctor Tyson's phone on the counter. Breaking the kiss, Aiden exclaimed, "Somebody better be in some sort of danger!" Pulling away, he pulled out his phone and saw he had a missed call and voicemail from Alex. "I need to teach Alex the joys of texting." He started listening to the voicemail.

"There's some sort of robbery at a restaurant called Tuli," Doctor Tyson said, looking at his phone.

Aiden set his phone down. "That's the restaurant my brother is having his date at."

"I hope he's okay." Doctor Tyson sat his phone down, taking Aiden's hand in his. "Maybe he left before they got there."

Aiden smiled wickedly. "For their sakes, I hope so."

"What are you doing after lunch?" Aspen asked, slowly moving his hand across the table to grab the check.

Yawning, Gaymer quickly snatched the check. "Zoink! Too slow."

"I asked you here." Aspen pursed his lips. "I should pay."

Gaymer slipped a card into the checkbook. "True, but why should either of us pay when my uncle can?"

"Your uncle is okay with that?" Aspen asked curiously.

Gaymer covered his mouth as he yawned. "I don't know, and I don't care."

"He's an asshole," Chitter said, poking his head out of Gaymer's bag on the floor.

Aspen laughed. "I'm really beginning to like that squirrel." When Gaymer yawned again, he asked, "What time did you go to bed last night?"

"Not too much later after we finished gaming." Gaymer wiped at his eyes.

Chitter made a squawking sound. "He didn't go to bed until three in the morning."

"Thank you, Chitter." Gaymer pushed the robotic squirrel back down into his bag. "I had to work on something for my uncle, which is why he is paying for our meal." He handed the check to the server. "After this, I was going to take Chitter to the park, but it seems my squirrel friend is really a rat."

Aspen smiled when Chitter poked his head back out of the bag. "Don't blame them because you didn't get any sleep. Maybe we should skip gaming tonight. We can talk on the phone or something instead."

"Scared I might beat you?" Gaymer teased.

Aspen crossed his arms over his chest. "You have yet to beat me."

"Only because Chitter keeps helping you." Gaymer yawned again. "I really should get some coffee or an energy drink to keep me going."

"You need to go to bed and get some sleep," Aspen scolded him. "And Chitter doesn't help me." Aspen winked at the squirrel. "What did your uncle have you doing so late at night?"

Gaymer took the check from the server. "Thank you." Adding a generous tip, Gaymer signed the slip. "He had me working on some stupid toys for his puppies."

"Puppies?" Aspen questioned. "Why would he have you working on toys for puppies until three in the morning?"

The conversation in the restaurant went quiet. The customers and staff were shocked and puzzled by the four men in tight jeans and black shirts wearing Pup hoods that busted into the restaurant.

They were each brandishing a strange-looking gun that had what appeared to be a megaphone where the barrel was.

"Nobody move!" The lead Pup shouted. "Hand over all your money and valuables and no one will get hurt."

Gaymer recognized two of the Pups as the ones that tried to catch Chitter. He snatched his bag with Chitter off the floor and pushed it toward Aspen. "Take Chitter and head into the back."

"I'm not leaving you," Aspen said, taking the bag. "We'll give them what they want and we'll be alright."

"What do you think you're doing?" The squat, heavyset manager went storming up to the Pups. "You freaks! I've already called city security. They'll take care of you and your toy guns."

The lead Pup pointed his weapon at the manager and squeezed the trigger. A blue electrical bolt shot from the odd weapon and hit the manager in the chest. His body went rigid. Every single hair on his body shot straight out. The manager's body jerked and spasmed. He fell to the floor, twitching.

"Anyone else?" the lead Pup growled. No one said anything. "I didn't think so. Pups, fetch their valuables."

Gaymer reached out and grabbed Aspen's hand. "Please, I'll be okay, but they'll hurt Chitter if they see him."

"How do you know?" Aspen saw Chitter cowering down in the bag. "Fine, but be safe."

Gaymer squeezed Aspen's hand. "I will, and thank you." Gaymer galnced at the Pups going through the crowd. "I'll distract them, you run."

"Don't do anything stupid." Aspen let go of Gaymer's hand and clutched the bag close to his chest.

Gaymer winked. "Me? Never." Gaymer stood up. "Aww! Look at the cute puppies!" He walked away from the table. "Who wants a belly rub?"

"Gaymer." Aspen heard one of them snarl. Aspen dropped to the floor and began crawling to the kitchen. He heard the Pup growl, "Where's that little squirrel friend of yours? We want to play with him."

Defiantly, Gaymer reprimanded him, "Bad puppy! Bad! Bad! Bad puppy! Don't you make me hit you in the nose with a rolled-up newspaper."

"Chitter, who are those guys, and why do they want to hurt you?" Aspen asked once they were safely behind the kitchen doors.

Chitter popped its head out of the bag. "They are bad puppies. Gaymer thinks they won't hurt him, but they will. Brutus doesn't like him."

"Brutus?" Aspen questioned, standing up to peek out the tiny window in the door. He saw two of the Pups had their weapons pointed at Gaymer. Looking around the empty kitchen, he guessed the kitchen staff had escaped through the open back door. Looking sternly at Chitter, he told the squirrel, "You don't tell anyone what you see back here. Understand?"

Chitter cocked its head curiously. He put one paw where his heart would be and raised the other. "I promise."

Putting the bag on a nearby table, Aspen made a fist, then splayed out his fingers. A blue ball glowed to life on Aspen's fingertips. It rapidly traveled up his arm and over his body, transforming him into the sexy and dangerous Ice. She tapped a nail onto the glass, frosting it over.

"No one fucks with my man." Ice kicked the door open with her crystal and gold stiletto heel. All eyes, including the Pups went to her. "This restaurant has a strict no-animal policy." Ice formed a snowball and sent it flying at one of the Pups holding his gun at Gaymer, knocking him onto his butt.

The lead Pup turned his weapon on Ice. "Who do you think you are, Ice Princess?"

"I'm a queen, thank you, but you can call me Ice." An icicle formed in front of Ice. She tapped it and sent it flying at the lead Pup. It wedged itself into the center of the gun. Turning her attention to the people, she ordered them, "Everyone out the back." She swirled her hands, causing the air to shimmer with ice. "These puppies need obedience training."

People rushed past Ice into the kitchen. The lead Pup snatched a nearby woman. One of the two Pups that had Gaymer at gunpoint grabbed him, while the other held his weapon on Ice. The third Pup moved to stand by the lead Pup. The air in the restaurant began to chill.

"Back off, lady," the lead Pup snarled. "We've got hostages."

Ice smirked. "What you have is a problem with me." She crossed her wrists in front of her, then pulled them apart. Hailstones flew across the restaurant, hitting each Pup in the center of the forehead. With the Pups dazed, Gaymer and the woman broke free. Ice grabbed Gaymer as he rushed by with the woman. "Chitter is on a table in the back."

"How?" Gaymer asked, then stopped when he looked into Ice's eyes. "Thank you."

Ice winked at him. "Go on, I have some puppies to punish."

"Collar those bitches." Gaymer grinned, rushing into the back.

Ice turned her attention back to the Pups when she heard the lead Pup yell, "Get her!"

She turned to see the Pups staggering to their feet. The three with guns took aim. Ice raised her arms, bringing up a clear ice dome. The sparks hit the ice and dissipated. Ice brought the dome down, then shot precision icicles into the center of each of the guns, shattering them in Pups' hands.

"Are you boys ready to roll over and play dead yet?" The air in the restaurant grew colder. The windows frosted over. A thin sheen of ice grew from where Ice was standing and spread out across the floor. The Pups growled at her. "I guess not."

The lead Pup barked, "Get her!"

The Pups charged her, but slipped on the ice. They struggled to get up, only to be pelted by snowballs from Ice. "Oh, this is too much fun." She laughed, sending another Pup crashing into the floor. "Too bad I have to go back to work." Ice flipped her wrists up so her fingers were pointing to the ceiling. "It's time to crate you puppies."

Ice flicked her wrists down. Large six-foot-long icicles fell down from the ceiling, surrounding each of the Pups. Ice waved a hand, causing a sheet of ice to form over the top of each trapped Pup, sealing them in their ice cages. The Pups began howling in dismay.

Ice frowned at the sound of the sirens coming near. "That's my cue to leave." Ice blew them a frosty kiss. "Stay frosty boys." Ice turned and sashayed into the kitchen.

CHAPTER 20

SHADOW GUARDIAN WAS ABOUT TO leap to the next building when Shadow Voice ordered, "Shadow Guardian stop!" Pausing at the building's ledge, Shadow Guardian waited for Shadow Voice to continue. "The threat at the restaurant has been neutralized."

"City Security?" Shadow Guardian asked.

"No. Witnesses are saying it was…" There was a brief pause before Shadow Voice answered hesitantly, "An Ice Queen?"

Shadow Guardian cocked his head questioningly. "Did you say the threat was neutralized by ice cream?"

"Clean out your ears," Shadow Voice groaned. "I said Ice Queen, and that's not even the strangest part. Apparently, the perpetrators were Puppies."

Shadow Guardian put his hands on his hips. "Wait. The restaurant was being held up by cute little puppies? I'm a hero, not a dogcatcher."

"You're about to be both," Shadow Voice announced. "I'm getting multiple reports of robberies all over the city. One is directly below you at the Morgan City Bank." A Shadow Drone maneuvered to hover above Shadow Guardian. "Grab on."

Taking hold of the handles Shadow Guardian asked, "What am I dropping into?"

"Men in Pup hoods with some sort of shock guns." The drone spiraled down. "I've got three coming out of the bank now."

Shadow Guardian studied his display. "There's a fourth in a getaway car parked out front."

"I wish you had back-up." Shadow Voice's words were laden with worry.

Knowing he needed to inspire confidence in Shadow Voice, Shadow Guardian said, "I do have back-up. The best back-up. You. Now sling me over at that light post and I'll show you what I learned from the gymnast I dated for a brief stint."

"New rule." The Shadow Drone angled and increased speed. "No more mentioning exes."

Shadow Guardian let go of the drone, letting himself be slung at the light post. "Fine." He grabbed the light post. Spinning around it, he let go, sending him hurtling feet first at the entrance of Morgan City Bank and the three Pups that were rushing out. "Time to pound some puppies."

Shadow Guardian's feet struck the largest Pup in the center of his chest, sending the shocked Pup hurtling backward with his bag of ill-gotten loot. Kicking off the Pup, Shadow Guardian spun in the air back toward the street. He landed on the roof of the getaway car, caving in its roof.

"They won't get far on foot." A Shadow Drone zipped around the car to shoot darts into the tires.

Shadow Guardian looked around. A crowd was gathering. People had their phones out, filming him.

"It's Shadow Guardian!" someone yelled.

"I thought he only protected the Northside!" someone else called out.

"I guess I'm more popular than I thought," Shadow Guardian told Shadow Voice.

Someone then shouted, "I bet he's responsible for these freaks! Get him!"

"Not as popular as you might think," Shadow Voice chimed in. "Now focus. They have their guns pointed at you."

Shadow Guardian felt someone grab his ankle. He looked down to see the Pup that was driving had squeezed halfway out of the window and was trying to pull him off the car. Moving with lightning speed, Shadow Guardian twisted and punched the Pup in the nose. He heard a squeak as the Pup's head flew back, sending him tumbling from the car.

Turning and facing the other three, Shadow Guardian asked, "What was that squeak?"

"Apparently, some Pups put squeakers in their muzzles," Shadow Voice read over the com. "Man, how has my search history not put me on any watch lists?"

Leaping into the air to avoid the blasts from the three Pups, Shadow Guardian, said, "You were, but we got you taken off them."

"Great," Shadow Voice groaned. He grew serious. "Alegro just finished the analysis of their shots. They pack enough juice to short-circuit your suit. Avoid them at all costs."

Shadow Guardian threw a Shadow Star into the gun hand of one of the Pups and shot a tendril to snatch the gun out of another. "Gee, why didn't I think of that?"

"Don't be a smart ass." The Shadow Drone extended a grappler to catch the weapon that flew in the air, then zoomed to scoop up the other on the ground.

The largest of the Pups pointed at Shadow Guardian, then barked, "Woof!"

"Did he just woof at me?" Shadow Guardian prepared himself for the two charging Pups. "I thought people only did that on the apps."

Suspiciously, Shadow Voice asked, "Why do you know that?"

"I was single once, remember?" Shadow Guardian evaded one of the Pups' blows but was caught in the chin by the other. He punched one in the stomach, then did a quick uppercut to the other. One of the Pups sucker punched Shadow Guardian in the gut. Clutching his hand, he let out a howl of pain. "The new reinforced armor checks out."

Shadow Voice shouted in alarm, "Watch out! The big one is firing!"

"On it." Shadow Guardian grabbed the Pup that was holding his hand. He moved the Pup between him and the larger Pup. He let go of the Pup a moment before the shot hit him. He watched the Pup go rigid, then fall to the ground, convulsing.

The larger Pup tried to fire again, but nothing happened. He let out a menacing growl, then barked, "Woof!"

"We need to end this," Shadow Voice ordered. "The crowd is growing. People could get hurt."

From behind, the other Pup wrapped his arms around Shadow Guardian to try to keep him in place. The larger Pup charged him. "Are these two serious?" Shadow Guardian laughed. He put his hands on the wrists of the Pup that held him. "Shadow Voice, are you ready?"

"Ready." The Shadow Drone scooped up the last gun, then moved to hover ten feet in the air.

Shadow Guardian sent an electrical shock into the Pup holding him. The Pup let go with a cry of pain. Shadow Guardian slung the howling Pup around and into the crushed getaway vehicle. Then, with the flourish of a matador, Shadow Guardian stepped aside to let the larger Pup slam into the car.

"Ole!" Shadow Guardian said merrily.

The Shadow Drone zipped in, shooting the two groaning Pups with tranquilizer darts. "Need a lift, sexy?" The Shadow Drone hovered over Shadow Guardian.

"Only if you promise to respect my virtue." Shadow Guardian grabbed the handles under the Shadow Drone.

Lifting him up in the air to the cheers and jeers of the crowd below, Shadow Voice laughed, "What virtue?"

In the alley behind Tuli, Ice changed back into Aspen. He looked at a shocked Gaymer. "I know you have questions."

"What are you?" Gaymer asked in awe.

Ashamed, Aspen looked at the ground. "I don't know." Hugging himself, he said, "I understand if you don't want to see me anymore."

"Are you kidding?" Gaymer laughed. "You kick ass in video games and you kick ass in life! You're amazing!"

Aspen cracked a smile. He cautiously looked up. "You really think so?"

"Absolutely!" Gaymer closed the distance between them. Standing on his tiptoes, he kissed Aspen. "I've never been so turned on in my life."

Aspen laughed. "We're not having sex in a back alley." Aspen winked. "I am a queen."

"That you are. A kick-ass queen." Gaymer looked down at his bag. "I need you to do something for me. Something really important."

Concern seeped into Aspen's voice. "What is it? Are you in trouble? You saw what I did in there. Let me call my brother—"

"Take Chitter." Gaymer shoved his bag into Aspen's arms. "Protect him. When Brutus finds out I was here, he's going to try to hurt me by hurting Chitter."

The robotic squirrel popped its head out of the bag. "I don't want to leave you!"

"It's only for a little while." Gaymer rubbed the top of Chitter's head. "Aspen will take real good care of you."

Aspen looked down at Chitter, then at Gaymer. "I don't know what to do. What should I feed him? Where should he sleep?"

"He doesn't eat, silly. He sleeps on a charging pad." Gaymer looked imploringly into Aspen's eyes. "Do this for me, please. Chitter is my world. If anything happens to him…" Gaymer wiped away a tear. "I know you can do it and if you have him, it means I have no choice but to find you again."

Aspen shouldered the bag. "What do you mean, 'find me again?'"

"Chitter, be a good squirrel for Aspen," Gaymer said, ignoring Aspen's question. "Chitter, Omega Protocol."

Chitter let out a sad squeak. "Understood."

"I'll see you two again soon." Gaymer leaned up to kiss Aspen again. "I promise." Gaymer turned and ran down the alley.

Aspen called out after Gaymer, "Wait! What is Omega Protocol? Gaymer!"

"Omega protocol means I don't try to track him down," Chitter said mournfully in the bag. "It'll even stop me from helping other people find him."

Aspen reached in to pet the heartbroken squirrel. "Omega Protocol applies to you, not me." The ground around Aspen froze over. "Come on, Chitter. I have family that can help us."

"There are reports of men in Pup hoods robbing and looting the city." Aaron sat his phone down. "They are overwhelming the City Security, spreading them too thin."

Joshua slammed his fist down on the table. "I should be out there helping them."

"Thank you for calling, Dion. Let me know if you hear anything. We're on our way." Juan Carlos looked somberly at the two men staring at him. "Aspen was on a date at one of the restaurants that was targeted. They don't know whether he's safe or not."

Joshua stood up. "Then we need to find out."

"Aaron and I are heading to DJC to assess the situation." Juan Carlos motioned Aaron to stand with him. "As soon as we know something, we'll call."

Joshua scoffed. "Don't think you're leaving me here. I'm going."

"I said you're staying!" Juan Carlos proclaimed, standing.

Putting a hand on Juan Carlos's shoulder, Aaron asked, "If the situation were reversed, if it was Diego or Alex or Esmerelda or Freddy in this situation, would you not insist on going?"

"I wouldn't worry about them, not even Alex. They can protect themselves," Juan Carlos grumbled. "You're right, though. Come on Joshua. I'm sure Aiden will need your support."

CHAPTER 21

"SIR," KEAGAN NERVOUSLY stepped into Mayor Trainer's office, "there's trouble in the city."

With a casual air and a self-satisfied smile, Mayor Trainer turned to face his timid assistant. "Why are you telling me? I'm no longer the mayor, remember?"

"Yes, sir. I know, sir. It's just..." Keagan shuffled his feet and rubbed his hands together. "I didn't know if you wanted to make a statement."

Mayor Trainer shook his head. "No. I'll make my statement tonight during the debate. Is everything ready?"

"Y-yes, sir." Keagan looked at the picture he hung behind Mayor Trainer. "Do you like the picture I used to cover the hole?"

Mayor Trainer spun in his chair to inspect the photo of him with Gaymer. "It'll do for the debate, but after I'm married, I want my wedding picture with Brutus hanging there."

"Of course, sir." Keagan trembled at the mention of Brutus's name. "I'll, um, I'll go get your lunch ready."

Turning back around, Mayor Trainer woke his computer up. "Shut the door on your way out. I have an important video call to make." Keagan scurried out, closing the door behind him. "Pathetic scaredy cat."

Mayor Trainer clicked the video app and waited for Brutus to answer. He smiled brightly when he saw Brutus's handsome face appear on the screen. "I've missed you, my love."

"I've missed you, too." Brutus let out a soft whimper. "When can we be together again?"

Mayor Trainer put his hand on the screen. "Soon, my love. Soon. With your Pups terrorizing the city, the people will turn on Felipe Montoya and Aaron Heath. Have all the Pups returned?"

"All but two packs." Brutus swallowed nervously. "They were arrested. According to the news, Shadow Guardian foiled the bank robbery at Morgan City Bank and some Ice Queen put the Pups at Tuli on ice, literally."

Mayor Trainer slammed his fist down on the desk, causing the wood to splinter. "What?!"

"I'm planning on breaking them out tonight." Brutus shrank back on the screen.

Mayor Trainer calmed himself. "Do not do anything until I give the go-ahead. In the meantime, find me replacements."

"Yes, sir. I'll—" Brutus was knocked off-screen by an angry Gaymer.

Beating his fists against Brutus's massive chest, Gaymer shouted, "You evil asshole! How dare you send your Pups after me and Chitter!"

"I did nothing of the sort!" Brutus pulled Gaymer off him by the scruff of his neck. "Now calm yourself before I turn you into my personal chew toy!"

A piece of his desk broke off when Mayor Trainer slammed his fist down again. "Stop it, both of you!" Brutus let go of Gaymer. Gaymer stood angrily beside Brutus. "One of you, tell me what is going on."

"Oh, I'll tell you," Gaymer snarled. "I went on a date, and this jerk sent his Pups after me and Chitter!"

Defensively, Brutus exclaimed, "I did nothing of the sort! I didn't even know he had a date!"

"Then why did your Pups show up at Tuli where I was having my lunch date?" Gaymer accused, crossing his arms. "Oh, and when they saw me, why did two of the Pups want Chitter?"

Mayor Trainer sighed. "That was totally by coincidence. I chose where the Pups were striking. Not Brutus."

"Is that why they were after Chitter?" Gaymer stared coldly into the screen. "Remember what happens if anything happens to him."

Calmly, Mayor Trainer said, "I do. Brutus, did you tell the Pups that Chitter and Gaymer are to be left alone? That they are not to be harmed?"

"Yes, sir. I did." Brutus's voice shook.

Mayor Trainer's eyes grew hard. "Then why is Gaymer telling me Pups were after Chitter?" Brutus cringed at the question. "You are their leader! You are their alpha! Get the Pups in line and do it now!"

"Yes, sir, right away. I'm so sorry I disappointed you, sir." Brutus disappeared off camera.

Mayor Trainer's face softened. "Gaymer, tell me about your date. Who is the lucky young fellow?"

"Screw you." Gaymer ended the call.

Mayor Trainer nearly jumped out of his chair when he heard Dante speak. "You really should get your house in order if you expect to join the board."

"How did you get in here?" Mayor Trainer hissed at the young man lounging on his sofa.

Dante stretched and yawned. "I'm a demon twink, remember?"

"So you say." Standing up and coming around his desk, Mayor Trainer stood there, arms crossed. "What do you want, Twink?"

"Demon Twink," Dante corrected him. A sly smile spread across his face. "Why would I want anything from you when I already have an obedient husband that satisfies my carnal desires?" Dante made a loathing face. "Besides, I'm not into puppy play anyway."

"Either state your business or get out!" Mayor Trainer pointed to the door.

Getting off the couch, Dante grew serious. "Your bid for mayor is over. The people of this city hate you. They blame you and Brutus for what happened today. Bow out gracefully now, and you can still use your influence to get us what we want."

"Get out," Mayor Trainer said through clenched teeth. "Get out before I throw you out."

Dante stood. "Suit yourself." Dante brushed away the wrinkles in his shirt. "By the way, your assistant feels odd."

"He's a cat person," Mayor Trainer growled.

Dante thought for a moment. "Hhmm. Maybe that's it." Dante flashed a toothy grin. "Farewell." Dante snapped his fingers. Red smoke began billowing up from his feet, enveloping him. When it dissipated, Dante was gone.

CHAPTER 22

DIEGO LAUGHED AT ALEGRO swirling around him. "I missed you, too."

"Alegro really enjoys being here and helping." Alex couldn't help the warm smile on his face. "Alegro, let Papi change out of his suit. You can help me analyze these strange shock guns."

Alegro turned to look at Alex, then back at Diego. It jumped to the table and typed carefully on a small device. "Sorry, I like analyzing."

"It's perfectly fine." With the smile of a proud father, Diego tapped the center of his chest to retract his suit. "I secretly like analyzing things, too."

Alex pulled out the three shock guns from the drone. "Alegro, I don't want you touching these. They can short out your circuitry if they go off."

"Yes, Daddy." Alegro typed out. Turning to look at Diego, it then typed. "Why is Papi naked?"

Alex laughed. "Because he doesn't like to wear clothes under his suit."

"I'm wearing a jockstrap." Diego defended, grabbing his clothes off the table where he left them.

Alegro typed out, "That doesn't cover much."

"Trust me, it does." Alex winked at Diego, then put one of the guns in a tiny Plexiglas box. "It looks like these don't have a charge, but I'd rather be safe than sorry." Alex put the box in his 3D scanner. "This will give us a virtual working model we can work with."

Tucking in his shirt and doing up his pants, Diego asked, "Any word on Aspen?"

"Aiden said he's okay and on his way back to work." Alex started the scanner. "This will take a few minutes." Alex grabbed his tablet and tapped away. On the huge wall monitor, a map of the city came up. "These are all the places that were hit."

Tying his tie, Diego examined the map. "Those are all in the Southside. Nothing in the Northside was hit."

"I noticed that." Alex tapped away at the screen again. "They were also places that are frequented by high society. Restaurants, banks, and even an art gallery."

Diego straightened his tie. "The ones I fought only barked, err woofed. Did they speak at any of the other locations?"

"According to the reports, only one or two of them in the group actually spoke." Alex swiped up on his screen. "The rest communicated by woofing."

Alegro typed on his device. "Is that why they were wearing Pup hoods?"

"Your guess is as good as mine." Diego shrugged. "Ever since the Three Bears, we've had all sorts of strange criminals wearing masks."

Alegro's voice box announced, "I'll cross-check them all and see if, wait, someone's coming."

"Quick, in here." Alex opened a drawer beside him. Alegro lept in. "I'll leave the drawer cracked for you, okay?" Alegro made a thumb's up. "We have the best child."

Diego studied the map. "We do."

"Aspen!" they heard Dion shout just as Aspen came through the door.

Diego looked at the flustered man. "Aspen, I can't tell you how happy we are that you're alright."

"Are you alright?" Alex asked, concern crossing his face. "Do you need to sit down?"

Dion entered a moment later. "I'm sorry, guys. He insisted on seeing you, even though I told him to go home." Dion put a hand on his shoulder.

"You've been through a traumatic experience. We don't expect you to come back to work until you're ready."

"Aspen, that bag doesn't match your shoes." Alex moved to Aspen. "Why do you have it?"

Aspen turned and shut the lab door. "I know I'm not being myself right now." Aspen carefully placed the bag on one of the worktables. "I need your help. It's Gaymer."

"Gaymer?" Dion asked. "Your date? Is he okay?"

Aspen shook his head. "Yes? No? Maybe? I don't know."

Diego went to Alex's side. "Why don't you take a deep breath and tell us what you do know?"

"Gaymer had just paid the bill when those Pups came in." The air chilled around Aspen. "He was under the impression they were there for him and Chitter."

Dion asked, "Who or what is Chitter?"

"This is Chitter." Aspen opened the bag and lifted out the sullen squirrel. Holding Chitter to his chest, he said. "It's okay, Chitter. These are friends."

Diego reached out to pet Chitter but drew back his hand when it flinched. "Is that a robotic squirrel?"

"Yes." Aspen nuzzled Chitter. "Long story short, Gaymer made Chitter to be his friend, and they really haven't been apart since."

Alex leaned in to study Chitter. "Why do you have Chitter?"

"Gaymer gave him to me and made me promise to take care of it." A tear ran down Aspen's cheek, leaving a frozen sparkling trail. "Then he ran off saying that if I had Chitter, he had to find me again."

Dion gave Diego a worried look. "I don't think we're the right people to help you, Aspen."

"What I need is a charging pad for Chitter and for you to find Gaymer." Aspen's voice grew cold and dangerous. "I'll handle the rest."

Dion's voice was full of worry. "Aspen, you're not acting like yourself. Sit down, please."

"I have a charging pad Chitter can use." Alex rushed to his desk and pulled out one of his spare charging pads. Plugging it in, he said, "Here, let Chitter charge up while we talk."

Hesitantly, Aspen went over to Alex. To Chitter, he said softly, "It's okay. These people are my friends. They won't hurt you. I promise."

"I thought you said we were going to see your family. Is this your family?" Chitter asked.

Startled, Dion jumped back. "Holy fuck! It talks!"

"That is awesome!" Diego proclaimed excitedly.

Stroking Chitter, Aspen said, "Sort of."

"Yes, we are," Alex corrected. "That means your family, too."

Chitter looked at Alex curiously. "Gaymer is my family. If I'm your family, does that make Gaymer your family, too?"

"Yes, it does." Alex smiled at the tiny robotic squirrel. "And this family does whatever it takes to protect its own."

Aspen carefully put Chitter on the charging pad. "Thank you, Alex." He stroked Chitter from head to tail.

"He means it." Diego put his arm around Alex.

Coming up beside them, Dion leaned down to look at Chitter. "I'm sorry I jumped when you spoke. You just startled me, that's all."

"I know I can scare people sometimes, but they tend to like me when they get to know me." Chitter cocked its head, then turned to the drawer with Alegro in it. "Who is that?"

Confused, Aspen said, "There's no one there, Chitter."

"Yes, there is." Chitter ran off the table and jumped onto the table that Alegro hid in.

Alarmed, Alex shouted, "Chitter, don't open that!"

"Hi. I'm Chitter. Who are you?" Chitter asked.

Dion asked Aspen. "Was he damaged at the restaurant?"

"I don't think so." Aspen went to get Chitter, but Diego rushed by him.

Nervously, Diego said, "Maybe Alex should run a diagnostic on Chitter, make sure—" Alegro popped out of the drawer and started wrapping itself around Chitter. Defeated, he finished, "—he doesn't reveal our secret."

"What is that?!" Dion asked, pointing a finger at Alegro.

Aspen pushed Diego aside to rush to Chitter. "It's hurting Chitter!"

"No, it's not." Chitter laughed. "Alegro is nice. Alegro is family."

Dion took a seat. "I need answers, and I need them now."

"Let them play." Alex guided Aspen to sit beside Dion. "Alegro won't hurt Chitter." Looking at Diego, he asked, "How much should we tell them?"

Chitter squeaked in amazement, "Your Papi is Shadow Guardian! That is so cool!"

"I guess everything," Alex answered his own question.

Diego shook his head. "Alegro, secret identity."

"Boys, I need answers, and I need them now," Dion ordered.

Aspen looked at Diego. "You're Shadow Guardian?"

"Yes," Diego put his hand on Alex's shoulder. "And Alex is Shadow Voice. He runs the command center."

Dion took a moment to digest the information. "Does Juan Carlos know? What am I talking about? He knows everything."

"So who was the wolf that was with you when you captured the Three Pigs?" Aspen asked.

Alex put his arm around Diego. "It's not our place to say."

"Okay, so is that," Dion pointed at Alegro, "the child you were talking about at lunch?"

Guiltily, Diego said, "Yes." Squeezing Alex's shoulder, he said, "We forgot to use protection."

"Not funny, Diego." Dion scowled.

Alex shyly said, "It was a little funny." Alex shrank back at the angry look Dion gave him. "Okay, so I took the technology from Diego's suit and tweaked the artificial intelligence a little."

"Alex!" Dion shrieked. "We have protocols in place when it comes to artificial intelligence!"

Alex smiled weakly. "That's DJC, I work for JCA. Remember?"

"Is there anything else I should know?" Dion shook her head in disbelief.

Aspen stood up. "Aiden is going to yell at me for this, but the Ice Queen that stopped the robbery at the restaurant is me." Aspen clenched his hand, then opened his fist. The blue orb ran across his body, transforming him into Ice.

"I'm Ice." She spun around for everyone.

Aiden came in at that moment. "Hey, Juan Carlos is…" he paused. "Oh, we're doing this, huh?"

"Locks." Alex mused. "We need locks on the door."

Shutting the door behind him, Aiden said, "Since you've met Ice, I guess you should meet Fire."

Aiden snapped his fingers. The small flame rushed over him, transforming him. "I'm Fire," she said with a curtsey.

"Now the hair makes sense!" Diego exclaimed.

Dion threw her hands up. "We have twin superheroes on staff?!"

"We're not superheroes," Ice answered, swirling her hand and creating a small ball of ice.

Proudly, Fire said, "We're Drag Queens."

Dion pinched the bridge of her nose. "Can you, please, change back? And what was that about Juan Carlos?"

"He's on his way up with Aaron and Joshua." Fire snapped her finger. The flame returned to her finger, transforming her back to Aiden.

"Does he know about you two?" she asked, watching Ice turn back to Aspen.

He shook his head. "No, but Joshua does."

"Are you sure you can trust Joshua?" Alex asked. "He is in love with Teddy."

Aiden took a seat beside Aspen. "Oh, yeah. Totally. His other boyfriend is a Drus. We were going to help him find his boyfriends. That's why I had Doctor Tyson make that suit for him." Aiden winced. "That I didn't tell you guys about."

"Oh, wow, this is a full house," Juan Carlos said, coming in with Joshua and Aaron.

Dion narrowed her eyes at Juan Carlos. "How could you keep all this from me?"

"She knows." Alex moved so he could see Alegro playing with Chitter.

Diego sighed. "She knows everything and then some."

"Aye, dios mio." Juan Carlos shook his head. "What are you madder at? The Shadow Guardian thing or that Demona is half angel and half demon?"

Dion's eyes went wide with shock. "Demona is half angel and half demon!"

"I take it she didn't know that part." Aaron shut the door behind them.

Alex plopped down on a nearby stool. "Nope."

"I'm going to end up with a tail, aren't I?" Diego groused, shaking his head.

Juan Carlos gave Dion a big smile. "She's a wonderful person. You shouldn't hold what she is against her."

"Mythical creatures make great lovers," Joshua added.

Dion put her hands up. "Stop! Everyone!" The room grew silent. "What's next? Is Esmerelda really some Gitana with magical powers?" She saw Diego and Juan Carlos exchange worried looks. "She is?!" Dion stood and began pacing. "What about her boyfriend, Gato?"

"Oh, he's a cat." Dion shot Diego a dirty look. "No, seriously, he's an actual cat. You see—"

Juan Carlos cut him off. "Diego."

"Right, not important right now." Diego nodded.

Dion stood still a moment, one hand on her hip, the other hand holding her head. Looking up, she said, "Freddy is the wolf creature, isn't he?"

"Lunar wolf, actually," Alex corrected. "It's a very sad and sweet story," Dion glared at Alex, "that can wait for another time."

Dion fixed her gaze on Aaron. "What secrets are you hiding from everyone?"

"I was just as shocked as you are when I found out." Aaron put his arm around Juan Carlos. "I know it's a lot, but you'll get used to it."

Dion's eyes grew wide. "We have twin Drag Queen superheroes for personal assistants!"

"We're not superheroes," Aspen corrected.

Aiden boasted proudly, "We are fabulous, though."

"Excuse me?" Juan Carlos looked between Aiden and Aspen.

Joshua spoke up. "Go on, guys. Show them."

Aiden and Aspen stood and transformed.

"I'm Fire," she said with a flourish of flame.

Ice created a small burst of snow. "Ice."

"We have the coolest family!" Chitter barked merrily.

Juan Carlos looked at Diego and Alex. "Did that squirrel just talk?"

"That's Chitter," Ice answered.

Fire gushed, "Aww, he is totally adorable!"

"Okay, last thing." Dion took several deep breaths. "What is this about Fire or Aiden having Doctor Tyson make a suit for Joshua?"

Juan Carlos turned to look at Joshua. "Yes, what is this about you getting a suit made for you?"

"It wasn't my idea." Joshua held up his hands in defense. "Fire told me about her suit ideas after she shot fireballs at me when I was training."

Everyone looked at Fire. Lackadaisical, she said, "He dodged most of them."

"I'm dating a half-angel, half-demon." Dion collapsed back onto a stool in disbelief.

"I'm totally getting sent to a Hell dimension for this," Diego groaned. "Do you think she'll at least let me have conjugal visits with Alex?"

CHAPTER 23

MAYOR TRAINER LOOKED DOWN at the gathering crowd of people protesting in front of his home. It riled his anger to see the DJC City Security below, forming a barrier between his home and the angry citizens of Morgan City. He wouldn't need their protection if Aaron Heath and Diego Sanz hadn't intruded into matters that were none of their concern.

Ingrates! They don't know the sacrifices we've made on their behalf to keep them safe! Mayor Trainer stepped away from the window. *If this is how they are going to repay us, repay me, then they don't deserve to have me as their mayor!* Mayor Trainer sat at his desk. *Dante was right. It is time for me to end my campaign for mayor.*

He woke his computer, then called his fiancé. The screen came to life and one of his Pups was staring at him through the screen, looking worried. With a boiling anger in him, Mayor Trainer asked as calmly as he could, "Where is Brutus?"

The Pup looked away nervously, then back at him. "Woof."

"Woof?" Mayor Trainer looked at the Pup questioningly.

The Pup pointed off the screen and repeated, "Woof."

"Get your hands off me!" Gaymer could be heard shouting. "I will have you neutered!"

Brutus shoved the Pup aside and appeared on the screen, holding Gaymer by the scruff of his neck. "I'm sorry, sir. It came to my attention that Gaymer sabotaged the shock guns he made for us."

"I did not!" Gaymer squirmed in Brutus's grasp. "You had me working until three in the morning! What did you expect? I told you to test them, but did you listen? Noooo!"

Mayor Trainer exhaled loudly. "I will handle it when I get there." Both men looked at him, perplexed. "Send someone to pick me up from the secret entrance. We are officially ending our campaign."

"Yes, sir. It will be good to see you again." Brutus smiled. Shaking Gaymer, he asked, "What should I do with him?"

Mayor Trainer looked at his nephew. "Gaymer is under house arrest until further notice."

"What!? You can't do that!" Gaymer tried to pull away, but was snatched back by Brutus.

Mayor Trainer looked his nephew in the eye. "I can and I will. I want all those shock guns fixed and operational. We're going to teach this city to heel under my boot." To Brutus, he said, "I'll see you soon."

He ended the call. Pulling up a blank document, he quickly typed his letter of resignation and withdrawal from the mayoral campaign. Printing the brief statement, he looked to his door, where he knew Keagan was skulking about. He hated entrusting such an important task to such a pathetic underling, but he had no choice.

"Get in here, Keagan." Mayor Trainer ordered, carefully folding the paper and sealing it in an envelope.

The cowering young man stepped in. "I wasn't eavesdropping or anything, sir. I was coming to see you when —"

"I don't care." Mayor Trainer stood and handed Keagan the envelope. "You will read this on my behalf at the debate. Word for word."

Keagan trembled with nervousness. "You're not going to attend the debate?"

"You were listening at the door, you tell me." Pulling out a flash drive from his top drawer, he plugged it into his computer. He quickly opened the drive, then clicked on the skull and crossbones icon. The computer monitor went blank with an error message, then came the pop of circuits, then a small puff of smoke before the air was filled with the scent of burned circuitry. "It will be your last official duty as the mayor's personal assistant."

Stepping out of the back of the van in his worn denim jeans, black shiny boots, and black studded harness, Mayor Trainer smiled. His beloved Pup Brutus was there waiting for him in his bulldog harness, Doberman mask, and tight, black, shiny shorts and boots.

"Give us a kiss." Mayor Trainer pulled the man to him by the harness. "I've missed you."

Carefully lifting his hood, Pup Brutus said, "I've missed you, too." Putting his arms around Mayor Trainer, the two shared a sensual kiss. "What happened?" Pup Brutus asked softly.

"Protesters," growled Mayor Trainer. "The crowd kept growing and those fools from DJC didn't know how to handle it properly."

Pup Brutus grumbled, "They didn't have infiltrators to start a riot?"

"No." He pulled Pup Brutus close. "If it wasn't for that damn Felipe Montoya and Aaron Heath, we wouldn't be in this mess."

Pup Brutus nuzzled his head against Mayor Trainer's chest. "What are we going to do?"

"For starters, we're going to get Gaymer in line." Mayor Trainer stroked his lover's back. "Then we're going to send the Pups out to cause chaos this city has never seen before."

Pulling back, Pup Brutus sniffed the air. "What is that smell?"

"Brimstone. Isn't it lovely?" Dante appeared from around the van, flanked by two of his muscle minions. "Doug Trainer, I've come to offer some assistance."

Pup Brutus growled, "That's Mayor Trainer."

"Not anymore." Dante cackled with delight.

Mayor Trainer stopped Pup Brutus from attacking the demon twink. "He's right. I'm just Trainer now." He looked lovingly into Pup Brutus's eyes. "Your Trainer."

"Oh, how sweet." Dante yawned. "Are you through with the lovey-dovey? I'd like to get home to my husband sometime this century."

Pup Brutus snarled, "What do you want, Twink?"

"That's Demon Twink," Dante corrected with an impish smile.

Trainer pushed Pup Brutus behind him. "State your business, Dante. We're busy."

"I've simply come to offer some of my muscle minions to assist." Dante ran a casual hand along the cheek of the man on his left. "They aren't that bright, but they are obedient and effective in numbers."

Trainer eyed Dante with suspicion. "What's the catch?"

"No catch," Dante said with deceptive innocence. "Consider it a token of friendship. As is this." Dante swirled his fingers. A gold and silver bracelet appeared. "I've even made you something to keep that precocious Gaymer in check. I've enchanted this trinket to punish the wearer if they disobey its master." He sent the mystical jewelry over to Trainer. "The Board wants to see how this plays out."

Trainer snatched the bracelet out of the air. "And who is its master?"

"Why, you, of course." Dante quietly added, "For now."

Trainer eyed the bobble. "This won't hurt him, will it?"

"No more than necessary to ensure he obeys," Dante answered casually. "You have to break a few eggs to make an omelet."

Trainer tossed the bracelet back. It landed with a metallic clack at Dante's feet. "No." He looked around, then at Pup Brutus. "Where is Gaymer, anyway?"

"He's locked in one of the hypno-rooms." Pup Brutus took a step back when he saw the anger on Trainer's face. "We had no choice. He kept trying to escape."

Knowing what Pup Brutus said was true didn't lessen Trainer's anger. "Stay here with Dante. I'm going to get Gaymer and then we're going to settle this stupid feud between you two."

"Take your time." The bracelet rose to float in front of Dante. "I've been wanting to get to know the fiercely loyal Pup Brutus."

Taking Pup Brutus's hands in his, Trainer looked imploringly into his lover's eyes. "Don't trust him. He's a demon."

"Demon Twink," Dante corrected.

Trainer ignored the correction. "Their help comes at a high price." He put his forehead to Pup Brutus's. "You and Gaymer are prices I'm not willing to pay. Understand?"

"Yes, sir," Pup Brutus answered softly.

Trainer kissed Pup Brutus softly on the lips. "I'll be back in a moment."

Trainer reluctantly left his lover with the Demon Twink, but he needed to deal with Gaymer. He navigated through the warehouse and its hastily set up base of operations. Pups moved to the side and smiled happily at him as he passed. He treated them each with a, "Good boy."

He went straight to the hypnotic chamber with two burly Pups standing guard. "Open the door."

"Woof." The one on the left nodded and opened the door.

Gaymer sat crossed leg in the center of the room, shooting death glares at him. "Leave us," Trainer ordered.

"Woof." The other Pup responded before the two headed off.

Gaymer's voice was filled with anger. "Is this the new ultimatum? Obey or get turned into a Pup like the rest of your servants?"

"Gaymer, I knew nothing of this." Trainer stepped into the room. He offered his hand to help Gaymer up, but he swatted it away. "I'm here to get you out of here. Then you, Pup Brutus, and I are going to hash out this feud you two have going on."

Gaymer pushed himself up off the floor. "Feud? He hates me! He has ever since I moved in!"

"He doesn't hate you." Trainer put a hand on Gaymer's arm, but he pulled away. "He's a Pup. He's my Pup."

Gaymer rolled his eyes. "What does that even mean?"

"He's jealous of you. Jealous that I pay you attention instead of him," Trainer explained.

Gaymer crossed his arms and tapped his foot. "Your little kink game isn't an excuse for him to be an asshole to me."

"It's not a kink game!" Trainer took a moment to center himself. "It's a lifestyle. One we choose to live. It allows Pup Brutus to bring out a part of him that he can't when he's not in Pup mode. If you gave him a chance, you would see." This time, when Trainer put his hand on Gaymer's arm, he didn't flinch away. "Put forth an effort. I'll make sure Pup Brutus does, too. I want us to be a family."

Gaymer looked up at his pleading uncle. "I will."

"Thank you. Now I need you to fix those shock guns you developed for us." As an afterthought, he asked, "Oh, and can you tell me why my Pups are woofing instead of talking?"

Gaymer gave him an incredulous look. "Really? You don't know why?" He sighed when Trainer shrugged. "You're brainwashing them to be pups, not human Pups. They are losing their humanity and becoming nonverbal."

"Is there any way to reverse it?" There was a hint of compassion in Trainer's voice that Gaymer wasn't used to hearing. "I wanted human Pups, not puppies."

Gaymer shook his head. "I don't know. That's out of my league."

"Will the gloves you made me have the same type of effect?" Trainer pressed.

Gaymer hesitantly said, "Yes."

"Good." Trainer grinned. Putting his arm around Gaymer, he started walking his nephew out. "Why don't you show me our new toys?"

Pup Brutus appeared in the doorway. "Dante left. He's sending us his muscle minions."

"Good." Trainer nudged Gaymer forward. "Gaymer, don't you have something to say to Pup Brutus?"

Gaymer chewed his lower lip a moment, then stuck out his hand. "You're going to be my uncle's husband, and I want us to be friends. No more hostilities."

"I'd like that." Pup Brutus took his hand. Gripping it tightly, he used his other hand to snap Dante's bracelet onto Gaymer's exposed wrist. "Dante's little trinket will make sure you keep that promise."

Gaymer yanked back his hand. He tried to pull the bracelet off. "What is this? Get it off!"

"Pup Brutus, what did you do?" Trainer knocked his lover aside. Kneeling down, he tried to pull the bracelet off Gaymer. "You heard me tell Dante no to this!"

Pup Brutus put a hand on Trainer's shoulder. "I did what you wanted to, but couldn't."

"Gaymer, I'm so sorry." Trainer pulled his nephew into a hug. "I'll get Dante to remove this, I promise. In the meantime, I need you to fix those pulse guns."

Gaymer pushed his uncle away. "I'm not doing anything for you!" The bracelet glowed. Gaymer screamed and fell to the floor as pain shot through his body. "What was that?"

"Obedience insurance." Pup Brutus grinned triumphantly.

CHAPTER 24

ALEX SAT WITH ASPEN WATCHING Chitter and Alegro play in the lab. Sensing Aspen needed reassurance, Alex said, "We'll find Gaymer and get him back."

"You're not going to let us help, are you?" Aspen asked, never taking his eyes off Chitter.

Alex looked at the robotic beings playfully chasing each other. "That's not my call, but probably not."

"We've had our powers since we were thirteen years old." When Aspen spoke, each word came out with a frozen puff. "We can control them."

Needing to distract Aspen, Alex asked, "How did you two get your powers?"

"Our mother is a geologist." The nip in the air around them faded. "She didn't know she was pregnant with us when she was studying this strange meteorite."

Chitter and Alegro stopped playing. Chitter jumped onto Alex's lap while Alegro swirled himself into Aspen's lap. "We want to hear the story, too." Chitter chirped, whipping his tail excitedly.

"Okay." Petting Alegro gently, Aspen smiled down at them before continuing. "She took every precaution, but the strange radioactive energy must have seeped through, into us. She said it was like it was there in the rock and then it was gone."

"They tested her." Aspen looked back up at Alex. "That's how she found out she was pregnant. They tested us too until we were five, but they didn't find anything."

Curiously, Alex asked, "What happened when you turned thirteen?"

"Don't laugh." Aspen's lips curled slightly into a smile. "Aiden and I were fighting over a doll. Hard to believe, right?"

Chitter squeaked, "Not really."

"Go on." Alex laughed.

"Anyways," Aspen continued. "We were fighting over the doll and there was this explosion. He was all fire and I was all ice. It was the first time we transformed. We didn't change into our Drag personas at the time. That came later, as we learned to control it."

Alex nodded. "What did your parents think? Coming out gay is one thing, but coming out super?"

"They kept us home for a long time because they were scared we'd transform in public and get taken away," Aspen explained. "We eventually showed them we could control it and they let us go back to school, but we weren't the same kids. Aiden was outgoing, and I was cold, obviously."

Flicking its tail back and forth, Chitter said, "You're not cold. You make Gaymer warm in several areas. Some I'm not allowed to talk about because it's inappropriate."

"Chitter, you're going to fit right in here." Alex laughed. "Now if you could only help me figure out why those Pups aren't talking or how those pulse guns work."

Chitter turned around in Alex's lap and stood up on its hind legs. "Mind control. They are becoming nonverbal. I also have the designs for the shock guns and the special earpieces to block the mind control in my memory files. Do you want me to show you?"

"Are you serious?" Alex held Chitter to his chest as he stood.

Alegro flew off Aspen's lap to its voice box. The robotic voice asked, "Is Chitter in trouble?"

"Chitter isn't in any trouble. He might have just saved the day." Alex set Chitter on his workstation. He picked up his tablet and held it to Chitter. "Can you connect to this tablet?"

Chitter studied the tablet. "Done."

"Chitter, how do you have that information?" Aspen came over to stand by Alex.

Chitter ran its paws together. "Gaymer didn't tell you?" It cocked its head at Aspen. "He made the guns and fixed the mind control machine for his uncle."

"Chitter." Alex tapped away on the tablet. Doctor Gingerman's hypno-box design came on the giant wall monitor. "Is this the mind control machine?"

Chitter studied the screen. "It was. Gaymer changed it. Here." The screen changed with Chitter's file upload. "That's it now. It's smaller, and he made two portable ones for his uncle."

Nervously, Alex asked, "Chitter, who is Gaymer's uncle?"

"Please, don't hate him, Aspen," Chitter pleaded. "His uncle is Mayor Doug Trainer."

Aspen picked Chitter up and hugged him. "Why would I hate him for who he's related to?"

"Because he made those guns for the Pups, too." Chitter changed the screen. The specifications for the pulse guns came on the screen. "He did sabotage them by not charging them fully."

Alex studied the screen. "We need to get Diego and Juan Carlos down here." Alarms started blaring. "What now?"

"Diego, you put me in an awkward position," Dion said, looking out the window behind her desk.

Diego shifted uncomfortably in his seat. "I know it can be a bit much finding out about me being Shadow Guardian. Aaron got drunk when he found out."

"I couldn't care less about that." Dion spun around and fixed Diego with a look. "I'm talking about Demona being half demon and half angel. How could you set me up with someone like that?"

Diego relaxed. "Oh, that. I really didn't think about her being a mixed mystical when she asked me to introduce you two. Haven't you two had a wonderful time together?"

"We have." Dion's face brightened.

Diego leaned forward. "Then what's the big deal? I'm sure she would have told you when the time was right."

"I do like her," Dion smirked. "You're also scared of her, so there's another plus."

Diego pleaded, "Please, tell her it wasn't me that told you."

"Don't worry, I'll tell her it was Juan Carlos." Dion leaned back in her chair. "What we need to worry about are the three want-to-be superheroes in the building."

Diego leaned back in his chair. "According to Aiden and Aspen, they aren't superheroes. Joshua says he just wants to save his boyfriends."

"All three want to help you find Gaymer," Dion added. "You can't let them."

"I'm not going to," Diego said firmly. "They don't have the training or skills to be out there."

Dion nodded. "Good. Now we need to discuss your child."

"What about Alegro?" Diego instantly went on the defensive.

Dion kept her tone calm and even. "You know the protocols about artificial intelligence. You're the one that put them in place after that incident."

"Then I need to revisit them," Diego said curtly. A moment later, he said a little calmer, "Alegro is fully realized and sentient. Our protocols cover the development of, not the existence of, artificial intelligence, not to mention Alex technically works for JCA."

Dion responded sharply, "That's a loophole and you know it." Sitting back in her chair, she sighed. "You're right though. Alegro is already here, and I won't give the order to end a life. We do need to decide how we're going to handle it."

"Remember, what we decide for Alegro is going to apply to Chitter, too." Diego started laughing. "If you could have seen your face when Chitter spoke."

Dion burst out in laughter. "He is totally adorable."

"They," Diego corrected. "Just because it's programming in binary, doesn't mean Chitter is."

Dion bowed her head in acquiescence. "I stand corrected. I should have known better than to assume pronouns." The DJC alarms started going off. Dion jumped up from her seat. "What now?"

Joshua leaned against Aiden's desk. "How much trouble do you think we're in?"

Aiden tapped rapidly at his computer. "For me? No more than usual."

"Juan Carlos was pretty mad to hear you had a suit made for me." Joshua pushed off the desk and began pacing. "You're not going to get fired, are you?"

Aiden giggled. "What? Me? No. Maybe. I don't know." Aiden thought for a moment. "Probably not. You don't fire the guy that can literally set fire to the whole building."

"You wouldn't." Joshua turned and saw Aiden's mischievous grin. "Will you take this seriously?"

Aiden moved his hands from the keyboard. Naughtily he asked, "Do you want to see it?"

"See what?" Joshua eyed him suspiciously.

Aiden pulled out a small box from his desk. "Your suit!"

"Put that away," Joshua ordered. "We're in enough trouble as it is."

Aiden rolled his eyes. Putting the box back in his desk, he huffed, "You're no fun."

"How are we going to help Aspen if they won't let us?" Joshua put both his hands on Aiden's desk. "They don't know what we can do, and they won't let us show them."

Aiden snapped his fingers and created a flame. "Technically, Aspen and I did."

"Put that out before someone sees." Joshua tried to snuff the flame out with his fingers, but Aiden kept it lit. "Aiden."

Aiden extinguished the flame. "Fine." Aiden brightened when he saw a message pop up on his screen. "Hey! Do you think I should tell Doctor Tyson about my abilities? You saw how freaked out Dion got when she found out about Demona."

"Maybe you should wait until you two actually go out on a date or two first," Joshua snarled.

Aiden's eyes went big. "I am so sorry! Here I am talking about my love life when you're still heartbroken because we haven't found your boyfriends! How insensitive of me!"

"I'm okay with you having a love life, or the beginnings of one." Joshua shook his head. "I'm worried they aren't going to let us help them find Gaymer or going to help me find Teddy and Jack."

Aiden pulled the box back out. "We don't need their permission."

"I said put that away." Joshua started pacing the office again. Feeling Aiden's eyes on him, he said, "I'll try it on when we get home."

Aiden put the box back. "I can't wait!"

"Excuse me." A young, slender blonde woman in a designer business suit strolled past Joshua. "I was told I could find Juan Carlos and Aaron Heath here."

Aiden stood up. "You must be from the campaign. They are right in here waiting for you." Aiden knocked on the door, then opened it for the woman.

"Thank you," she said, stepping past Aiden.

Shutting the door, Aiden asked, "Can you man the phones while I check on Aspen?"

"Sure." Joshua resumed his pacing. "It's not like I've got anything better to do, like battling supervillains."

Sitting on the couch in Diego's office, Juan Carlos held Aaron's hands. "Thank you for not telling our secret back there."

"I almost did." Aaron laughed. "Dion is scary when she's upset."

Juan Carlos pecked him on the cheek. "My brave hero."

"Actually, I was terrified Diego was going to start calling me daddy," Aaron teased. "When are you going to tell him? I want to see my ring on your finger."

Juan Carlos patted his hands. "Let a lady enjoy her engagement privately for a while." Juan Carlos ran a hand through Aaron's hair. "I want to tell Diego and Felipe together."

"What about your other children?" Aaron asked.

Puzzled, Juan Carlos said, "I don't have any other children."

"Yes, you do." Aaron squeezed Juan Carlos's hand. "Alex, Dion, and now Aspen, Aiden, and Joshua." Aaron thought for a moment. "I'm not sure how Chitter, Alegro, Esmerelda, Freddy, and Salvador fit in. We may need a flowchart."

Juan Carlos laughed. "It won't help."

"Probably not." Aaron grew serious. "What are we going to do about your three new heroes/want-to-be children?"

Juan Carlos waved his hands wildly about. "Oh, when they want to be superheroes, they're my children!"

"Fine, our children." Aaron laughed, pecking Juan Carlos on the lips. "What are we going to do about our children?"

Juan Carlos shrugged. "We're going to love and accept them. Then we train them. They're going to do it whether we want them to or not. At least this way we can give them the skills and resources to do it right."

"I don't like it, but you're right." Aaron sighed. "I wish Esmerelda and Gato were here to help. When are they coming back?"

Juan Carlos turned and settled back into Aaron. "Gato didn't know. Esmerelda was in a meeting with the Gitano council. I told him about the Rage seed and of the Pup attacks." He patted Aaron's hand on his chest. "He said they'd try to get ahold of Freddy to come back and help, but who knows if he can."

"We're on our own then." Aaron pulled Juan Carlos closer. "Do you think we should tell Felipe about Diego's alter ego?"

There was a knock on the door before it opened. Juan Carlos sat up quickly. "I don't know."

"Gentlemen." A young, slender woman with long flowing blonde hair stepped through the door. "I'm Mari. Mari Posa from Felipe's campaign." She didn't wait for either of them to speak. "The official decision about the attacks is that we are not to address them and if anyone asks, we are to answer with no comment."

Shocked, Juan Carlos jumped up. "What? That can't be right."

"I'm afraid it is." Mari adjusted the strap of the purse that dangled off her shoulder. "Since the criminal vigilantes got involved." Mari wrinkled her nose. "Shadow Guardian and that Ice Queen, it would be seen as condoning their actions and we can't have that."

Aaron stood, looking at his phone. "Are you sure about that?"

"Of course," Mari said with a confident smile. "I was told by Felipe himself. I'm not sure why he had me come all the way down here to tell you, but here I am."

Aaron showed Juan Carlos his phone. "Really?" He narrowed his eyes at the woman. "Who are you?"

"Mari Posa from Felipe's campaign office," she answered, confused. "Didn't I explain that when I entered?"

Aaron showed her his screen. "Then why did I get a text from Felipe saying he's sorry that he's just now sending someone to brief us fully on how we're going to praise Shadow Guardian and the Ice Queen for doing their civic duty?"

"Who are you really, chica?" Juan Carlos grabbed her arm. "Are you working for Doug Trainer?"

Mari gave them a sympathetic look. "Whoops! Guess my cover is blown." She yanked her arm back and did a spin, kicking Aaron in the chest with her six-inch heel. She yanked her blonde wig off and tossed it into Juan Carlos's face. "Nighty night boys!" She pulled a small spray bottle from her purse and spritzed a dazed Aaron and furious Juan Carlos in the face.

"What..." Juan Carlos staggered about, shaking his head, "was that?"

Watching Aaron fall over, Mari pulled out a lipstick from her purse and ran it over her lips. "Knockout spray. Very powerful."

"Puta madre." Juan Carlos dropped to his knees.

Mari's features changed. Her hair grew into an auburn pixie cut. Her features grew sharp and angular and the suit she wore turned into a pair of jeans and a crop top. Her shoes morphed into a pair of stylish sneakers. "Don't worry boys, they didn't pay me to kill you. You'd be dead if they had." Juan Carlos collapsed onto the floor beside Aaron. She turned to the door. "See ya."

Stepping out of the office, Mari was slipping the lipstick back into her purse right as she collided with a pacing Joshua. "I'm so sorry." Joshua picked up the fallen lipstick. He looked into the open office and saw Juan Carlos and Aaron on the floor. "What happened?"

"Oh, nothing." Mari tried to snatch the lipstick from Joshua. "You know old people, they need naps."

Joshua held the lipstick out of her reach. "You're not the same woman who went in there." Joshua read the label of the lipstick. "Murderous Red." Anger rose in him. "Where did you get this?"

"Honey, you have two choices. Hand me the lipstick and get out of my way or I take the lipstick after I kick your cute ass." Mari held her hand out. "What's it going to be?"

Stepping back, Joshua wrapped his hand around the lipstick. "Where's Teddy?"

"Teddy? You mean the scraggly bear in the woods?" She cocked an eyebrow. "I just got paid to get and deliver him. What they did with him after that is none of my business." Mari raised her fists, ready to fight. "Now hand over the lipstick."

Joshua mirrored her stance. "Not until you tell me where Teddy is!"

"Oh, you think you can take me?" Mari threw a punch. Joshua grabbed her by the wrist. "Nice move." She stomped on Joshua's foot.

Joshua let go of her. "Bitch!"

"I've been called a lot of things in my life." Mari did a roundhouse kick, but Joshua jumped up onto Aiden's desk to avoid it. "Give up, sexy. You'll never beat me."

Joshua lunged at Mari, tackling her to the ground. "Where is Teddy?!"

"Give me back my lipstick!" Mari wrestled with Joshua, moving so she was on his back, with her legs wrapped around him and her arms around his neck, trying to choke him out. "Give up!"

Joshua slammed his head back into her face. "Where's Teddy?!" He pulled himself away from her and got back to his feet. Wiping a trickle of blood from his lip, he watched the woman's broken nose snap back into place on its own. "What are you?"

"I'm Lip-Sync." Her face morphed into a young man with a scar that ran across his left cheek. One cruel eye was black, the other milky white. "The Assassin."

Tackling Lip-Sync, Joshua shouted, "Did you kill him you freak!"

"Normally, I love having a man on top of me." Lip-Sync brought her knee hard into Joshua's groin, sending the man rolling over in pain. "Unfortunately, this time I have to take a rain check." She stood up and snatched the lipstick from Joshua's hand. "Catch you later, cutie."

Joshua grabbed her ankle. "You're not going anywhere."

"Oh, yes, I am." She reached into her purse and pulled out the knockout spray. "Nighty night." She prayed Joshua in the face. Joshua's hand fell away from her ankle.

Juan Carlos groaned from the floor. Watching Lip-Sync strut away, he reached into his pocket and pulled out his phone. "Hija de puta." He pressed the alarm on his phone. Lip-Sync glared back at him, struggling to get up off the floor. She applied the lipstick, morphing her features into a muscular black man wearing a DJC security guard uniform, then casually walked away.

CHAPTER 25

"HOW COULD YOU?" TRAINER asked the cringing Pup Brutus. "We have rules in our relationship."

Pup Brutus kept his eyes downcast when he softly said, "Yes, sir."

"Pup Brutus," Trainer lifted his lover's head. "When I found you locked in that kennel by that cruel man, what did I do?"

Pup Brutus's eyes watered. "You rescued me."

"That's right." Trainer ran a thumb along Pup Brutus's cheek to wipe away a tear. "He beat you. Starved you. He had you living in your own filth." Trainer smiled. "I brought you back to my place. I washed you. Fed you. Tended to your bruises. I gave you a soft bed to sleep in. I held you when you had your nightmares. I did everything I could to get you to trust me."

Choked up, Pup Brutus said, "I fought you every step of the way."

"You did, but I didn't push, did I?" Trainer pressed his forehead to Pup Brutus's. "You eventually trusted me."

A warm smile spread across Pup Brutus's face. "You were watching a show on the couch. I came in and sat on the floor, across the room from you."

"It took you an hour, but you slowly inched your way over to me." Trainer ran a hand over his fiancé's head. "You eventually got up on the couch and snuggled me."

Pup Brutus's voice was choked up with emotion. "I was so scared you'd reject me."

"Never." Trainer wiped a falling tear from Pup Brutus's cheek. "Remember what I asked you?"

Pup Brutus took a deep breath to calm himself. "You asked what I wanted."

"And?" Trainer asked.

Pup Brutus straightened his posture and looked at Trainer with determination in his eyes. "I told you I wanted to be safe, be protected, be strong, be loved, and never put in a cage ever again."

"Did I not promise you all that?" Trainer asked. "All I asked in return was that you never betray me."

Hurt filled Pup Brutus's face. "I never betrayed you."

"What you did to Gaymer." Trainer pulled away from Pup Brutus. "You know he's the only family I have besides you."

Pup Brutus hesitantly reached out to Trainer. "He disobeys you. He challenges you. He makes you look weak in front of the pack."

"He is not one of my Pups!" Trainer shouted, harsher than he intended. "Even if he was, I'm the Trainer! I'm the leader! It is my place to discipline, not yours!"

Pup Brutus instinctively dropped down to his knees and lowered his head. "I am sorry, Trainer. I was only trying to look out for you. I did not mean any disrespect. Please, forgive me."

"Do you know what Dante wants?" Trainer asked, his chest heaving with anger and fear. "He wants Gaymer. I will not lose him. Do you understand me? I will not lose him."

Pup Brutus looked up, his face growing hard with determination. "I'll protect him for you. Let me do that for you."

"And lose you both?" Trainer caressed Pup Brutus's face. "No, have two of our most loyal and strongest betas stand watch with him. I want you by my side tonight."

Pup Brutus nodded. "What is the plan?"

"I want Dante's muscle minions in the audience of the debate. When Keagan reads my announcement, I want them to start causing chaos and take Felipe and Aaron." Pup Brutus nodded at Trainer's instructions. "We'll start by destroying Southside, starting at the Riverfront." Trainer's nostril flared. "Morgan City will pay for turning its back on us."

Pup Brutus stood. "Shall I prepare the Puppy Pack?"

"Yes, and I'll go tend to Gaymer and see if I can smooth things out with him." Trainer let out a defeated sigh. "I don't think he'll ever forgive you for this."

Pup Brutus hugged Trainer, needing to feel the comfort of his touch. "I won't stop until he does."

"Go now. Tonight we show this town who really runs it." Trainer patted Pup Brutus on the back. "Prepare the Pups."

Pup Brutus hugged Trainer tighter before pulling away. "I won't fail you again."

Trainer nodded. He watched a defeated Pup Brutus leave with his shoulders hunched over. *If you only knew the trouble you got us into.* Trainer left the tiny office and headed straight to Gaymer's workroom. The Pups gathered around Pup Brutus at the other end of the warehouse. He could hear them woofing their cheers at Pup Brutus's words.

Opening the door to Gaymer's workroom, he saw his nephew sitting with his back to the door at one of his workstations with wires attached to the cursed bracelet. He could tell by Gaymer's fingers punching the keys, he was getting more irritated by science's lack of explanation on the mystical charm.

Crossing the room, Trainer put a hesitant hand on Gaymer's shoulder. "You're wasting your time. It's magic, not science."

"There's no such thing as magic." Gaymer's voice was full of fear and hurt. "When I get this off, I'm going to put it around Pup Brutus's neck and see how he likes it."

Trainer spun Gaymer around in his chair. He saw the strain of tears Gaymer had fought not to cry. "Listen to me for once in your life." He took Gaymer by the shoulders. "This is magic. That demon twink, Dante, tricked Pup Brutus into putting that on you."

"Seriously, you're expecting me to believe in magic and demons?" Gaymer snorted. "You're a fool."

Trainer leaned down to look Gaymer in the eyes. "I'm not kidding and if you don't get those shock guns up and working properly, I'm not going to be able to keep him from getting what he wants." Trainer pulled Gaymer off his seat and into a hug. "You."

"Please, don't make me." Gaymer pleaded, hugging his uncle back. "Can't you all just turn yourselves in and we end all this?"

Trainer held his nephew tight. "We've gone too far to turn back now, and with that bracelet on you, I'm not sure how far we'll go."

"Then promise me you won't hurt Ice." Gaymer demanded in a choked sob. "You hurt her, and you and I are over."

Trainer rubbed Gaymer's back soothingly. "Does she mean something to you?"

"She's the protector of my world," Gaymer answered cryptically.

Trainer kneeled down to look his nephew in the face. "Then I will give the order that she is not to be harmed." Trainer thought for a moment. "I thought you were into boys."

"Who said she's not?" Gaymer wiped his eyes. "I'll fix the shock guns under one condition. You get this damn bracelet off me."

Trainer hoped his words didn't come out as uncertain as he felt. "I will. I promise."

CHAPTER 26

"HURRY UP!" AIDEN SHOUTED AT Joshua through the closed door. "I want to see what it looks like on!"

Alex paused the video recording of the fight outside of Diego's office. He zoomed in on Lip-Sync's morphing face. "Who or what is she?"

"Didn't your demon friend have any answers?" Aspen asked, keeping a surreptitious eye on Chitter lounging on the charging pad Alex put out for him.

Alex turned away from the screen. "She's half demon, half angel," he corrected Aspen. "No, she didn't. There are shapeshifters in the mystical world, but none like what this Lip-Sync did."

"It looks fabulous!" Aiden screamed when Joshua stepped out in his costume. "I need to take a picture to show Doctor Tyson!"

221

Alex jumped up and rushed to snatch the phone from Aiden's hand. "No pictures in here!"

"Oh, right. Secret lair and identities and stuff." Aiden shrugged. He ramped up his energy again. "But doesn't he look great!"

Joshua stood there in the black tight pants with a white stripe up the sides that accentuated the muscles in his legs and a formfitting, black, sleeveless V-neck collarless shirt that showed off his hard rigid muscles. "I feel so stupid in this."

"Put on your mask," Alex ordered, handing Aiden back his phone.

Joshua pulled out the domino mask and put it on. "It doesn't help."

"Isn't he forgetting the gauntlets?" Aspen asked, joining them. "And where is his belt?"

Joshua groaned at the three young men that simultaneously crossed their arms at him. "Fine, but I don't see why we're doing this." Joshua grabbed the belt and gauntlets from the other room. Putting them on, he said, "There's no way Juan Carlos is letting me go out and fight crime."

"He's the one that told me to have you try on the outfit." Alex winked at Joshua. "He's telling Diego you three are going to train to be superheroes."

Coldly, Aspen said, "I'm not a superhero."

"If you want to save Gaymer, you're going to be." Alex started moving around Joshua. "Okay, I see it. What code name are we giving you?"

Joshua looked at Aiden. "Did we decide on a code name?"

"Sentry," Aspen answered.

Alex checked the charge on the belt, then the gauntlets. "Okay, let's test these babies. Boys, can we have Fire and Ice join us for a bit?"

"My pleasure." Aiden snapped his finger, igniting his flame of change.

Aspen's blue ball of transformation appeared on his fingertip. "If I must."

"Wait." Joshua watched the two transform. "Can't we start out with something less dangerous, like water guns?"

Alex stepped out of the way. "I need to monitor their effectiveness under real fire." Alex sat down at a nearby workstation. "First Fire, then Ice. Then both of you together."

"I'm going to end up freezer burned." Joshua activated his protective shields and held his arms in front of him. "Are you sure Juan Carlos okayed this?"

Fire's flame hit the shield. "Wow, Doctor Tyson really did a good job on these, barely any energy loss at all."

"So we're done, right?" Joshua asked nervously.

Ice's frost blast hit the shields before Joshua could lower them. "Wow. It looks like he somehow is using the kinetic energy of the blast to recharge the gauntlets."

"Does that mean we're done?" Joshua saw Fire and Ice smiling at each other. Raising his shields again, he braced for the next attack. "Oh, shit."

Fire's and Ice's twin blasts swirled around each other as they crossed the room to hit Joshua's shield. "Ladies, that's enough." Alarms started going off on Alex's consoles. "Ladies! Stop before—" The shields sent a pulse of energy back at Fire and Ice, knocking them on their asses. "It sends back a feedback pulse," Alex finished.

"I didn't know it could do that." Joshua went over and helped Fire and Ice to their feet. "Did you?"

Alex tapped away at his screen. "No." He looked over to Alegro's charging vase, then to Chitter on his pad. "It looks like they've been altered by our two little mischief makers. That kinetic charging function is what I came up with for Diego's suit a few months back, and it's not in the DJC files. Chitter must have hacked the files when they uploaded the specs for those earpieces."

"Did they really alter the gauntlets?" Aspen asked, changing back.

Alex tapped at his screen. "No doubt. It's all over the programming. I recognize some of this code as the same Gaymer put in your phone."

"Are we upset that they made them better?" Aiden asked, as his transformation flame ran over his body.

Alex kept studying the screen. "Yes, and no. I want to know when they had the time to do this. We only left them alone with the gauntlets for a short time."

"Can I get out of this clown outfit already?" Joshua asked, pulling on the tight fabric. "I look ridiculous."

Aiden smacked his hand away from tugging at the garment. "It does not. It looks fabulous."

"It actually does." Aspen came over to admire the costume. "Aiden is a fantastic designer. He designs all of our clothes."

Alex pulled a small bag and a large disc from one of the wall compartments. "Why are you a personal assistant instead of studying design?" Handing the items to Joshua, he said, "These are for you."

"I tried to get into design school, but they said my designs were too flamboyant for them." Aiden twirled for them. "Can you believe they said I was too flamboyant?"

Joshua fumbled with the items Alex gave him. "What are these?"

"I tell you what, why don't you design me a new wardrobe? That way I can get Diego to stop sneaking the clothes he buys me into my closet." Alex returned his attention to Joshua. "In the bag are two discs that you can hurl at people."

Joshua took the tiny discs out of the bag. "So two and I'm done?"

"No, you'll see when you practice. They'll come back to you." Alex took the large disc back from Joshua. "Stand on this. It should be able to hold your weight."

Joshua stepped on the disc. "What do you mean 'hold my—' Whoa!" he shouted when the disc floated up in the air.

"You should be able to control it by shifting your weight. The disc has a magnetic lock on your boots to keep you from falling," Alex explained. "Try it out."

Joshua leaned forward slightly. He screamed, "How do I make it stop?!"

"Lean back!" Alex shouted, sitting down.

Taking a seat beside Alex at the workstation, Aspen asked, "What's wrong with Diego buying you clothes?"

"Okay, I think I'm getting the hang of this!" Joshua yelled as he started zipping around the room. "This is fun!"

Alex wrinkled his nose. "I love him, but Diego's tastes are good for Diego. They aren't me."

"I'm thinking of something contemporary, but with flair." Aiden sat down on Alex's other side. "Something simple, but not over the top."

Joshua stopped his air disc right in front of them. "How do I get off this thing?"

"Lift one foot up at a time," Alex answered.

Stepping off the air disc, Joshua asked, "What are we talking about?"

"Clothes and boys." The three of them answered in unison.

Joshua thought for a second. "I wear one and like the other."

"Pull up a chair," Aspen said with a rare smile. Turning to Alex, he said, "So you love Diego?"

Alex's eyes went big. "I did say that, didn't I?"

"You did!" Aiden took Alex by the shoulders and shook him playfully. "Have you said it to him yet?"

Shocked, Alex shook his head. "No. He hasn't told me he loves me yet."

"You love Diego!" Aiden drew a flame heart in the air with his index fingers.

Aspen patted Alex's hand. "He's said it, just not in words. I've seen the way he looks at you. I'm surprised he hasn't asked you to marry him yet."

"I just agreed to move in. That way we both could be here for Alegro." Alex looked over at Alegro. "He said he'd let me propose."

Pulling a stool over to the workstation, Joshua said, "You should both say I love you to each other before you propose."

"I wasn't going to propose," Alex clarified, sternly. "Okay, let's talk about your men now."

Joshua was the first to speak. "Even though Teddy kidnapped me with the other bears, he was different. He wasn't like the other two. I found out from Jack that Teddy had this Rage seed in him that was trying to drive him mad, but he was fighting it for me."

"How did you and Jack become an item?" Aiden asked, intrigued.

Joshua laughed. "He took care of me when I fell and hurt myself in the woods. When he saw I wasn't going to stop until I found Teddy, he started training me." Joshua smiled fondly at the memories. "Let's say it was unexpected since I was determined to win Teddy from him, but a casual touch here, a look there."

"Naughty," Aspen playfully chided. "You all know how I met Gaymer. I probably wouldn't be dating him if Alex hadn't told me to take a chance. He ignites this passion in me."

Alex looked over at Aiden. "Your turn."

"There's not much to share." Aiden shrugged innocently.

Joshua covered his mouth and faked coughed, "Bull shit."

"Fine, I like him. When I talk to him, he doesn't try to dumb down things because he thinks I won't understand." Smiling, Aiden hugged himself. "I feel very centered and tranquil when I'm around him." A shocked expression exploded on Aiden's face. "Wait."

Aspen's face mirrored Aiden's shock. "The old woman that came to see us after our powers emerged."

"What old woman?" Joshua's eyes darted back and forth between Aiden and Aspen.

Focusing on his brother, Aiden said, "I totally forgot about her until right now."

"I did, too." Aspen closed his eyes in concentration. "She came over, rubbed our foreheads with some smelly oil, and said she gifted me with passion and you with tranquility."

Aiden raked his nails through his hair. "What was her name?"

"She said she was a queen." Aspen held up a finger in the air. "Queen of the he something."

Alex suggested, "Queen of the Gitanos?"

"Yeah, that's it." Aiden snapped his fingers. "Madame Zelda, Queen of the Gitanos."

Questioningly, Aspen asked, "How did you know that?"

"This isn't our first rodeo with Madame Zelda," Alex shook his head. "We need to tell Esmerelda about this."

Joshua asked, "Didn't Dion mention her today? Who is she?"

"She's fabulous, a fantastic cook, and the most powerful person I know," Alex said with a smile. "She is the Gitana."

"No!" Diego said vehemently, pacing the room. "We are not training them."

Juan Carlos shouted back from the couch he sat on with Aaron, "What are you going to do then? Let them go out there without any training or support?"

"Guys, can I—" Aaron started to ask.

"It's dangerous! What if they get hurt?" Diego countered.

Rubbing his temples with his fingers, Aaron tried to ask again, "Please, could I—"

"It's just as dangerous for you." Juan Carlos crossed his arms. "Aspen's new boyfriend is in trouble. Joshua has two missing boyfriends. Aiden, well, Aiden is Aiden, but you get the point. They have loved ones they want to rescue."

Aaron patted Juan Carlos's knee. "Baby, could you, please—"

"That doesn't mean we should train them. If anything, it means we should be discouraging them from being superheroes." Diego stopped pacing and crossed his arms over his puffed-up chest. "I won't allow it."

Falling back onto the sofa, Aaron groaned. "Would someone, please—"

"You won't allow it?" Juan Carlos jumped up from the couch. "Are you forgetting who the Mamacita is around here?"

Diego looked shamefully at his feet. "No."

"Diego, I let you train and become Shadow Guardian because I knew if I didn't help you, you'd find a way to do it on your own." Juan Carlos stepped to Diego and lifted his chin. "If I hadn't helped you, you would have probably ended up dead. That's why we need to train those three. They're going to do it no matter what we say."

Diego hugged Juan Carlos. "I'm sorry for yelling, Mamacita."

"You're passionate, like your mamacita," Juan Carlos teased, hugging Diego back. "We need to take care of our family."

Groaning from the couch, Aaron asked, "How about one of you take care of me, or don't I qualify as family yet?" Juan Carlos and Diego turned to look at him. "Can I, please, get some aspirin? My head is throbbing."

"I'm so sorry, mi amor." Juan Carlos dropped to his knees in front of Aaron. "Diego, make Aaron that special healing tea Esmerelda left us."

Diego rushed to the kitchen, saying, "On it."

"I feel like I've been hit by a freight truck," Aaron moaned.

Juan Carlos patted Aaron's knee. "I know. Luckily, I held my breath after she sprayed you, otherwise, I'd be in the same condition."

"The tea is seeping. Here, take these in the meantime." Diego handed over two aspirin and a bottle of water.

"Thank you." Aaron quickly slammed back the two pills and chased them with the water.

Returning to the kitchen, Diego called back, "Are any of us surprised that the captured Pups are all police officers being looked for by Internal Affairs?"

Juan Carlos returned to his seat by Aaron. "Not at all."

"They were Chief Brutus's elite force. Now it makes sense he called them the pack," Aaron commented. "They were in every police station, and I think he still has some in there we don't know about."

Diego came back with a steaming cup. "What is with the Pup thing?" Diego sat the cup down in front of Aaron. "It is a bit weird."

"Not really. As Pups they can foster the power and strength that's inside of them." Juan Carlos picked up the cup and blew on it. "It's no different than you becoming Shadow Guardian or me as Dolores Salvaje." He handed the cup to Aaron. "Drink."

Diego sat down. "I didn't think about it that way, and if Chitter is right about them being mind controlled, then they don't know what they are doing."

"What is in this?" Aaron coughed, making a bitter face.

Juan Carlos pushed the cup back up for Aaron to drink. "Don't ask."

"It'll have you feeling refreshed for the debate tonight." Diego stood and stretched. "I don't know why we're even having a debate."

"The people still want to hear from the candidates." Aaron downed the last of the tea and began to gag. "My God, that's awful."

"But it works." Juan Carlos took the cup and set it on the table. "Diego should go get Alex and get ready."

CHAPTER 27

STANDING IN THE BACK OF THE empty box van, Trainer flexed his left hand, trying to get used to the feel of the fingerless glove Gaymer made for him. *Left is obey. Right is nothing.*

Trainer ran a hand over the inlaid quartz crystal on the back of his hand that told the small emitters in the palm of his hand what subliminal command to send. The sound of the back doors opening brought him out of his thoughts. He watched his beautiful Pup climb in and close the doors behind him.

"The Pups and Dante's muscle minions are all in place and are awaiting your command." Pup Brutus cocked his head curiously at him. "Is everything okay, sir?"

Trainer took Pup Brutus's hood off his head. "I need you to talk to me like my lover and not my Pup."

"What is it, baby?" Brutus took his lover in his arms.

Putting his arms around Brutus, Trainer asked, "Are we doing the right thing? Have we gone too far? Am I letting my pride endanger the Puppy Pack?"

"I wish I could tell you no." Brutus rested his head against Trainer's bare chest. "It doesn't matter now. The Pups are armed and ready to take this city down for you, and we have Dante's muscle minions out there. Who knows who they will really obey."

Trainer rubbed Brutus's head soothingly. "Whatever happens, know that I love you."

"I know." Brutus snuggled closer. "You are my world, Doug."

Trainer's lips curled into a soft smile. "It's been so long since I've heard you say my name." Trainer's hand glided down Brutus's back. "I should have married you years ago."

"We can't change the past, but we can make a future for ourselves together." Brutus gave his fiancé a gentle kiss. "Maybe we could disappear after this is all done? We can find someplace secluded and live out our lives together."

Trainer let out a humorless laugh. "I wish we had that option."

"We could walk away from all this, give the command and we go back, get Gaymer, and head out of town while the city burns." Brutus squeezed Trainer tighter.

Trainer gave his lover a reassuring pat on the back. "If only it were that simple. When Dante tricked you into putting that bracelet on Gaymer, he knew he was ensuring our obedience. No matter where we go, he'd find us."

"I'm sorry for being so foolish," Brutus cried softly into Trainer's chest. "It's all my fault."

Trainer lifted his lover's head up and wiped away the tears. "He tricked you. That's what demons do. If anyone is to blame, it is me for accepting their offer of help all those months ago."

"Then I guess there's only one choice." Taking his hood from Trainer, Brutus pulled away. Putting it on, his Pup persona emerged. "We're doing this."

Trainer nodded, pushing away his doubt. "We're doing this. As soon as Keagan makes the announcement, our Pups destroy the city."

"I know I've told you this already," Diego took his seat beside Alex in the crowded auditorium, "but you look fantastic."

Alex pecked him on the cheek. "Aiden really is talented. Can you believe he designed and made this entire outfit?"

"Maybe DJC should start its own design house and have Aiden head it up." Diego thought for a moment. "No, never mind. That means I'd have to get a new personal assistant, and we'd be back to Code Diegos."

Alex shifted in his seat to speak quietly into Diego's ear. "Something's been bothering me. Didn't you say you destroyed the motherboard for the hypno-device Doctor Gingerman made?"

"And the hard drive with the programming." Diego looked at Alex with concern. "How did Gaymer get a working one, then?"

Alex nodded. "Exactly. I've seen that programming. It's complicated. There's no way Gaymer could have come up with the exact same data programming as Doctor Gingerman."

"We'll need to find Doctor Gingerman and question him." Diego settled back in his seat.

Alex wrapped his hand in Diego's. "At least Chitter gave us the designs for special earpieces to block the effects." Alex looked around, then whispered into Diego's ear, "You did bring your suit, right?"

"Of course." Diego gave his hand a squeeze. "I never leave home without it."

"Are you okay?" Demona wasn't sure if she should reach out to a stunned Dion or not. "I'll understand if you never want to see me again. I can talk to Esmerelda about wiping your memory."

Dion's face went from stunned to hurt, then to anger. "Did you seriously ask me that?!"

"I only wanted to give you your options." Demona looked down at the table. "Dating outside of the mystical realm is new to me."

Dion laughed softly. "Dating a half demon, half angel is new to me, too." She reached out and took Demona's hands in hers. "I guess we'll figure it out together."

"Good." Demona gave Dion an uncharacteristically shy smile. "You know, when I saw that picture of you on Diego's phone, I knew I had to get to know you."

Curiously, Dion asked. "Which picture was that?"

"You were flying down the hall on some contraption." Demona laughed. "Then he showed me the video, and I knew right then that I had to know a woman who trusted Diego enough to do something as wild and crazy as that."

Dion rolled her eyes. "I don't know how, but he can get me to do the wildest and craziest things. The fact that he is Shadow Guardian doesn't even surprise me."

"He is a brilliant and utterly wacky pretty boy." Demona shook her head. "You know he was trying to get Ryuu to fly him and Alex around?"

Dion looked at Demona questioningly. "Fly him around?"

"Oh, I thought they told you." Demona cringed. "Ryuu is an asexual dragon."

Dion's eyes went wide. "Isn't he dating Andrea? Does he know?" Dion shook her head. "Of course he does."

"He does. They are an odd pair, considering Andrea is a unicorn." Demona smirked.

Dion grew excited. "I don't know how to process that. On the one hand, he's a unicorn." Excitedly, she said, "On the other hand, he's a unicorn!"

"Everyone loves a unicorn," Demona teased.

Looking over at Ryuu setting up the bar, Dion asked quietly, "How is it that he looks like, you know, a person?"

"Magical charms," Demona answered. "The mystical beings that cannot pass for human have magical charms that sort of transform them into the appearance of human, sort of like what Freddy has to ease his transformations."

Dion thought for a moment. "Isn't that, I don't know, demeaning?"

"In order to survive, you sometimes have to pass for something you're not." There was hurt in Demona's words. "The world of humankind can be a cruel and dangerous place for those of us that are different."

Dion nodded. "Don't I know it."

"Finding people who accept us like Diego, Alex, Juan Carlos, and Aaron have is a rarity." Demona smiled lovingly at Dion. "I'm glad you're one of those rare people."

"Please, don't hate me, but I have to ask because you're half-demon, half-angel..." Dion paused before hesitantly asking, "Do you have wings or a tail like the stories say?"

Demona's eyes went mischievous. One flashed white, the other red. "Both."

"You guys didn't have to stay home with me." Aspen was sitting on the couch, casually petting

Chitter. "You could have gone to the debate with the others."

Aiden looked up from his book. Alegro was wrapped around him, reading over his shoulder. "Meh. I'd rather hang with you guys than sit on uncomfortable chairs in a stuffy auditorium." Alegro turned the page. "Hey, I wasn't done with that page yet."

"I was thinking." Joshua came out of the kitchen with a big bowl of popcorn.

Cheekily, Aiden said, "Is that why I smelled something burning?"

"Funny." Joshua tossed a handful of popcorn at Aiden. Alegro quickly shot tendrils out to catch each kernel. "That was impressive." Alegro gathered them together and formed a small bowl on its side for Aiden. "As I was saying." Joshua sat down beside Aspen. "Chitter's Omega command keeps him from finding Gaymer, right?"

Chitter turned its head curiously at Joshua. "That is correct."

"It doesn't prevent you from telling us where the Pups are hiding, does it?" Joshua asked.

Aspen exclaimed. "Joshua, you're a genius!"

"Words not said too often," Aiden joked. Alegro shoved popcorn into Aiden's mouth.

"Alegro says be nice," Chitter translated.

Aspen picked Chitter up to look it in the eyes. "Does the Omega Protocol prevent you from telling us where the Pups are hiding out?

"Let me check." Chitter's eyes glazed over. "No, it doesn't."

He swallowed the popcorn. "What good is knowing where the Pups are?"

"Don't answer that," Joshua ordered quickly. "Not until Chitter tells us where they are."

Chitter chirped, "They are at Fetch Warehouse."

"Chitter, I love you." Aspen hugged it close.

Standing up, Joshua ordered, "Suit up, boys. We've got a rescue to mount."

"Oh! I get it! The Pups have—mmmphh," Alegro covered Aiden's mouth before he could finish the sentence.

"We don't want Chitter having some paradox error," Aspen explained.

Alegro removed his tentacle from Aiden's mouth and patted him on the head. "Who is going to keep an eye on these two while we're gone?"

"I'm a big squirrel," Chitter boasted proudly. "I can take care of myself."

CHAPTER 28

GAYMER PACED THE SMALL CONfines of his makeshift bedroom. His uncle claimed the two vicious-looking Pups standing guard outside his room were there for his protection, but the way they looked at him gave him an uneasy feeling. He didn't recognize them from his uncle's pack and they had a strange look in their eyes.

Get off! Gaymer futilely pulled at the bracelet. *Damn you, Brutus!*

The door swung open and the two guard Pups stepped through. "What do you want, mutts?"

They looked at each other, then back at Gaymer. The one with the purple hood pulled out lipstick and applied it around his snout. Gaymer jumped back in shock as the Pup's body and clothes contorted and twisted until they were rearranged to a svelte blonde woman in a form-fitting, white bodysuit.

The Pup in the green took hold of its head and snapped his own neck. He fell to the floor only to stand back up a moment later, also transformed into a voluptuous woman in a black and purple bodysuit with blue hair that fell around her shoulders. The smile she flashed at Gaymer sent fear down his spine.

"What the fuck are you?!" Gaymer shouted, moving away from them.

The purple-haired woman grinned while the blonde laughed and said, "My dear, what we are is none of your concern." She waved her hand in front of herself. "However, you may call me Lip-Sync, the Assassin." She waved her hand in front of her partner. "This is my protégé, Death Drop." Death Drop did an overly dramatic bow. "She doesn't speak much."

"W-what do you want?" Gaymer reached his desk. He felt around behind him for some sort of weapon.

The two stepped aside, and a young, slender, brown-haired man stepped forward. "What was promised to us by your uncle." Gaymer froze in fear. "You."

"I'm not going anywhere with you freaks!" Gaymer found a screwdriver and thrust it out in front of him like a weapon.

Dante rolled his eyes and waved his hand. "What are you going to do with that? Screw us?" Dante's eyes flashed red. "Do you not know who I am?" The lights flickered as Dante's words boomed in the room. "I am Dante! The Demon Twink!" He motioned to Gaymer. "Girls, bring him to me."

"Stay away from me!" Gaymer dropped the screwdriver and dashed to the right, only to have Death Drop land in front of him. Jumping back, Gaymer screamed, "Leave me alone!!"

Lip-Sync grabbed Gaymer's shoulders from behind. "Sweet little boy, make it easy on yourself and come quietly."

"No!" Gaymer turned, fist raised to strike, but fell to his knees from the agony the glowing bracelet shot through him.

Dante stepped forward and touched the cursed jewelry. "I am the true master of the bracelet. Not only will it force you to obey me, but it will not allow you to harm my agents."

"Wait until my uncle gets hold of you," Gaymer spat out when the pain subsided.

Crouching down, Dante stroked Gaymer's chin. "Naïve boy, who do you think promised you to us?"

"He would never," Gaymer cried out, clutching the offending bracelet as tears streamed down his face.

Dante stood, looming over Gaymer. "He did, and it was just a matter of convincing that stupid lap dog Brutus to put that bracelet on you when I sensed him faltering on our deal." He motioned to Death Drop and Lip-Sync. They lifted Gaymer up. "Let's go. I miss my Finn."

"I won't work for you!" Gaymer challenged. "I won't!"

Dante ignored Gaymer's protests as he led the group out of the small room and out of the warehouse. Once outside, he stopped. "What do we have here? More want-to-be superheroes?"

"I hope Diego won't get too mad that we took those other two hover discs." Fire crouched down with Ice and Sentry behind the dumpster. "They are fun to ride, though."

Itching to rush in, Ice flexed her fingers. "I don't give a damn if he gets mad or not. I want Gaymer back and I want him back now."

"We can't just rush in there." Sentry leaned the hover discs against the wall. "They could hurt Gaymer."

The ground around Ice began to freeze over. "We need to do something, and soon."

"He's right, Sentry." Fire's flames flickered on her fingertips. "We're here. What do we do?"

Sentry paused. "I'm not sure. Jack and I didn't cover actual infiltrations when I trained with him."

"Alegro says there are four heat signatures in the building." Chitter chimed in over their coms. A Shadow Drone whizzed by overhead. "They are making their way toward you."

Surprised, Sentry responded back. "Chitter, what are you two doing in Shadow Command?"

"Alegro is operating the consoles and I'm translating," Chitter barked back merrily. "Get ready. They are almost where you guys are."

Sentry stood. "Okay, Fire on my right. Ice on my left. Don't hurt any Pups unless you have to, remember they are mind controlled."

"No promises." A cold wind swirled around Ice.

Putting a hand on her shoulder, Fire said, "Remember, that's a line we don't want to cross."

"Fine." The chill in the air from Ice subsided. "How am I the hot-headed one and you're the cool and calm one?"

Fire shrugged. "Irony?"

"Alright." Sentry moved to stand twenty feet in front of the door. "Be prepared. We don't know what's coming out that door."

A slender young man in a business suit stepped out of the warehouse with two women dragging a struggling Gaymer with them. "What do we have here? More want-to-be superheroes?"

"Lip-Sync," Sentry growled when he saw the svelte blonde woman holding Gaymer. To Ice and Fire, he snarled, "The other two are yours. That bitch is mine."

The Shadow Drone dove at the three villains, letting loose a barrage of Shadow Darts. Dante swiped his hand, creating a magical shield. "Annoying little machine." With his other hand, he shot out orange blasts that the Shadow Drone narrowly evaded.

"Chitter, keep the Shadow Drone back," Sentry ordered. "When you see an opening, zoom in and grab Gaymer."

Chitter made a series of chirping and barking sounds. "Okay." The Shadow Drone rose in the air. "Kick their asses."

"Give us Gaymer and tell us where Teddy is," Sentry said, trying to make his voice sound as authoritative as he could.

Pretending to ponder it over, Dante cradled his chin and tapped his lip. "No." His eyes flashed red. "Lip-Sync, show these fools why they call you The Assassin."

"Gladly." Lip-Sync shoved Gaymer over to Death Drop. She strutted forward, pulling two silver fans from her back. Clacking them open, she revealed them to be razor sharp with the word "Slay" emblazoned in blood red across them. "Who wants to be my first victim?"

Taking the discs from his sides, Sentry stepped forward, poised to strike. "Me."

"Oh, it's you again, cutie. I'd recognize you any-where." A sinister smile spread over Lip-Sync's face. "It's a shame I have to ruin that pretty face of yours."

Lip-Sync spun, releasing one of the fans flying at Sentry. Raising his arms to activate his gaunt-lets, the shield activated just in time for the metal fan to bounce off it. Lowering his arms, Sentry hurled one of his discs at her. She effortlessly did a split, letting the disc fly over her head.

"I see you have new toys." Lip-Sync wiggled her fingers. Her fan came flying back into her hand.

Catching his returning disc, Sentry snarled, "You won't get away this time."

A fireball shot past Lip-Sync at Dante. He caught it with ease, but wasn't prepared for the icicle that followed it, hitting him in the chest. "Give us Gaymer and we might let you walk away."

Ice formed a dozen small hail stones around her. "This is your only warning, twink."

Annoyed, Dante said, "Demon Twink." He looked back at Death Drop. "Seriously, how hard is it to put 'demon' in front of 'twink?'" Death Drop shrugged. With eyes glowing red, he looked back at Fire and Ice. "Maybe I should show them so they don't forget."

Dante sent two orange magical blasts out, one at Fire, the other at Ice. Ice sent her hail stones around the blast at Dante, then spun away from the blast. Fire mirrored her move, then shot a barrage of flaming balls at the demon twink. Dante waved his hand, bringing up a protective shield that fizzled the flames and shattered the ice stones.

Taking advantage of the distraction, Lip-Sync threw a fan at Fire and one at Ice. Matching her speed with his quick flexes, Sentry slung his discs at the flying fans. The discs knocked the fans off course, skittering into the ground, then circled back for Sentry to catch.

Standing up, Lip-Sync spat out, "Bitch."

"That's my line." Sentry sent the discs flying at her before she could summon her fans back.

Lip-Sync curled one leg under her and fell back, narrowly avoiding the discs. Popping back up, she said, "We need to work on your aim, sweetie."

"Lip-Sync! Quit playing around!" Dante shouted, exchanging blasts with Fire and Ice. "Death Drop, hand me the boy! Take care of these heroes in heels!"

Shoving Gaymer into Dante's arms, Death Drop closed her hands into fists, then opened them. Her index fingernail grew ten inches in length. Making a gun with her hands, she aimed at Fire and Ice. With a maniacal laugh, she lowered her thumbs. Several razor-sharp nails shot out from her fingers at the twins.

Sentry charged Lip-Sync. The two dodged and blocked the other's hits and kicks so skillfully that they looked like they were doing an intricate dance rather than fighting. Meanwhile, Fire swirled her hands in front of her, creating a wheel of fire that melted the flying nails on impact.

Ice created an ice wall. The first three nails cracked and splintered the wall. The last one shattered it and flew by Ice's face, scratching her face and drawing blood. Ice put her hand to her cheek. Seeing the blood on her hand, her eyes flashed a cobalt blue. "You do not touch the face." Making a funny face, Death Drop stuck her tongue out at Ice. Ice raised her left foot. "You shouldn't make faces at people. They could freeze that way."

Ice stepped forward. The ground froze over at the touch of her blue, glass stiletto heel in a zigzag motion toward Death Drop. Death Drop looked at it curiously. She moved two steps to the left. The traveling ground ice changed direction toward her. She took four steps to the right. The traveling ground ice diverted to her. Death Drop let out an ear-curdling shriek, then took off running with the traveling ground ice chasing her around.

"Get her Ice!" Gaymer cheered.

Dante threw Gaymer to the ground. "Good help is hard to find." He raised his hands up. The ground began to quake and shake. A huge chunk of concrete lifted up. He sent the slab hurtling at Ice.

"Don't you hurt her!" Gaymer tried to tackle Dante but the bracelet sent him crumpling down to the ground in pain.

Fire sent a stream of flames at the hurling slab, sending it off course. "Didn't you hear my sister?" She moved to stand beside Ice. "You don't touch the face." Death Drop ran past them, arms waving frantically as the traveling ground ice chased her. Looking at Ice, Fire asked, "Can you just freeze her already? She's a little annoying."

"You're right." Ice double-tapped her foot. The ground ice chasing Death Drop sped up, catching her mid-step and freezing her in a shell of ice. "I hate overly dramatic queens."

Chitter chirped frantically in the three fledgling heroes' ears, "Guys, you need to finish this! The family is in trouble!"

"I'm trying, Chitter." Sentry threw a punch at Lip-Sync. She caught him by the wrist and tried to twist his arm around his back. Sentry countered her move, and they ended up with her back against his chest, pinned by Sentry's arm. Sentry growled, "Where is Teddy?"

Lip-Sync snuggled back against Sentry. "A girl could get used to being held like this."

"I'm not into girls." Sentry tightened his hold on Lip-Sync. "Where is Teddy?"

Lip-Sync slammed her head back into Sentry's face, causing him to stagger back and lose his grip on her. "Good thing I'm not really a girl then, huh?" She cartwheeled away with a wink.

"Let's show this twink... I'm sorry, Demon Twink," Ice mocked, "what we can do together."

Joining her hand with Ice's, Fire's eyes glowed volcanic red. "Chitter said to end this."

Raising their other hands, they aimed between them. A stream of fire and ice shot from their hands, joining between them. They swirled around each other and hit Dante's protective magical shield. It pulsed with the attack, and visible cracks began to form.

<Dante!> Finn cried out in Dante's head. *<We're under attack!>*

Putting his arms up to reinforce his shield, Dante sent back, *<I'm a little busy here.>*

<Doctor Gingerman's lab is under attack!> Finn continued in a panic. *<I need you to infuse me with more magical energy so I can defend it!>*

Dante pushed back against the sisters' joint attack. *<I can't. I have my own problem I'm dealing with. Do what you can. I'll deal with the fallout when I get back.>* Dante put a hand where the blast was hitting his shield. He sent an orange energy stream pushing back.

"I can't keep this up." Fire's flame stream grew weaker.

Ice squeezed her sister's hand. "You can do this. I know you can. You're stronger than you know."

"I'm sorry." Letting go of Ice's hand, Fire crumpled to the ground, exhausted.

Ice ended her attack and dove out of the way of Dante's magical blast. "It's okay." Ice held her hands palm up at her sides. "I've got this." The air grew colder. Ice began forming on every surface. The wind picked up. Shards of ice broke off and began flying around as Ice's blizzard gained strength.

Sentry crouched down and raised his shields to protect himself from the frozen bombardment. "Ice! What are you doing?!"

"She's going to freeze us, sweetie," Lip-Sync said into his ear. Crouching behind him, she commented, "I like a man that carries protection."

Dante looked at her, unimpressed. He snatched Gaymer by the arm and raised him up for Ice to see. "Stand down or he pays the price." To prove his point, Gaymer began to glow red and started screaming in pain. Dante reiterated, "Stand down."

"Stop it!" Ice lowered her hands, ending the blizzard. "Don't you dare hurt him!"

Dante dropped Gaymer to the ground. "I will dare what I will, my dear." Dante waved a hand, freeing Death Drop. She staggered, then shook her head. She stuck her tongue out at Ice before returning to Dante's side. "Ladies, we're leaving. We have urgent business back home. Death Drop, grab the boy. Lip-Sync, get our ride."

"Bye, cutie." Lip-Sync pecked Sentry on the cheek, then rushed off before he could grab her.

"You're not taking him." The wind started blowing again with Ice's anger.

Dante grabbed Gaymer by the wrist again. "He's a pocket gay. I wonder how he'd fare in a pocket Hell dimension."

"Ice, don't." Fire struggled to get up. Taking her hand, she said, "We've lost this battle. We'll get him back another way."

The Shadow Drone dive-bombed Dante. "I'm not losing him again." Chitter's voice came over their coms. Several darts shot out. They missed Dante and Death Drop, but one stuck in Gaymer.

"Machines." Dante groaned, hitting the Shadow Drone easily with one of his magical blasts and vaporizing it. "Now, if you three will excuse us, we have someplace to be." A black SUV driven by Lip-Sync pulled up. Furious, Ice and Sentry watched Death Drop push Gaymer into the back while Dante casually strolled to the passenger's side. Getting in, he smiled wickedly at them. "Until we meet again."

Once the door was shut, Lip-Sync sped away. Ice screamed, then fell to her knees. Frozen teardrops fell to the ground. "We were so close."

"I know." Fire hugged her sister.

Chitter piped into their ears. "I know it's not a good time, but Shadow Guardian and the others need your help. Pups are destroying the city, and they have Alex and Aaron."

"I know you're hurting but the city needs us." Sentry put a hand on Ice's and Fire's shoulders. "Are you up for it?"

Ice stood. She took Fire's hand. "Let's do this. Our family needs us."

CHAPTER 29

DIEGO PUT HIS ARM OVER ALEX'S shoulder and pulled him close. "Something's wrong," he whispered to Alex. "This was supposed to start thirty minutes ago."

"Here comes Juan Carlos," Alex whispered back, nuzzling Diego back. "We should talk covertly like this more often."

Diego turned so his lips brushed Alex's as he spoke. "We'll need lots of practice to get it right."

"If you two are done acting like a couple of teenagers," Juan Carlos put a hand on Diego's shoulder before crouching down, "we've had an unexpected development."

"Does Diego need to change outfits?" Alex asked cryptically.

Juan Carlos debated his answer. "Maybe. I don't know. We'll see how this plays out."

"What's going on?" Diego asked, leaning down to hear Juan Carlos better.

Juan Carlos checked to see if anyone else was listening before answering. "Apparently Doug Trainer dropped out of the race. He's having his personal assistant read a statement."

"If he's just reading a statement, why is it taking so long?" Alex asked.

Juan Carlos threw his hands up in annoyance. "He's as skittish as a stray cat. Every time they get him in place for the camera, he runs away."

"Can't someone else read it?" Diego asked.

Juan Carlos made a sound of annoyance. "He won't let anyone touch the envelope." The lights in the auditorium dimmed, then came back up. "It looks like they finally got him to stay behind the camera or they wrestled the envelope away from him." Juan Carlos stood. Looking around at the crowd, he said, "Stay alert. Something doesn't feel right."

"Maybe I should go back to Shadow Command, as a precaution," Alex suggested.

Juan Carlos studied the room. "Our junior team is there, and didn't you say Alegro knows how to run everything?"

"You trust Alegro to run everything? Aren't they technically a child?" Diego questioned.

Juan Carlos put his hands on his hips. "They've had more training than Alex did when you had him running it."

"Point made, but if anything happens, I want you two to head straight back to Shadow Command," Diego ordered. "I want you out of harm's way."

"Understood." Juan Carlos nodded. The lights flickered. "I should get back to Aaron."

The announcer came over the speakers as Juan Carlos hustled backstage, "Ladies, gentlemen, and non-binaries, may I present to you Felipe Montoya, candidate for mayor of Morgan City." Felipe came out. Waving to the crowd of cheering people as he headed to his podium.

"Due to circumstances beyond his control," the announcer continued, "our current mayor, Doug Trainer, is unable to be here." The announcer waited for the hissing and boos to end. "We do have his personal assistant," a screen lowered down, "Keagan Flowers, remoting in with a prepared statement from Mayor Doug Trainer."

A jittery, scrawny blond man appeared on the screen. "This is just a rehearsal, I promise." A woman off-camera could be heard saying. "Do it like you would if it were real."

"Okay." Keagan's hands shook as he opened the envelope and pulled out the letter. Unfolding the piece of paper, Keagan began reading with a shaky voice. "I, Doug Trainer, have served as mayor of Morgan City for four consecutive terms. Brutus Howard has served as the police chief for three of those terms." Keagan's hand dropped. "Can I start over?"

The woman off-camera could be heard saying, "This is just a rehearsal, keep going. I'll give you notes later."

"Okay." Keagan lifted the letter back up to read. "After all those years of faithful service, protecting, and doing what is right for the city, the city has turned its back on me and Brutus. You have no idea the sacrifices we've had to make on your behalf." Keagan cleared his throat. "As of today, I am withdrawing my candidacy for mayor of Morgan City. Let's see how your future mayor and police chief handle the upcoming crisis." Keagan dropped the letter. He looked straight into the camera and asked, "What upcoming crisis?"

In the auditorium, men began barking and howling. Diego and Alex looked around with the other confused guests. Random men were standing and putting on Pup hoods. People started screaming and running for the exits when the Pups began picking things up and attacking nearby people.

Diego grabbed Alex and tried to shield him from the stampeding people as they made their way to the front entrance. The entrance door flew open. There stood Doug Trainer in shiny black boots, worn jeans, a black harness, and two strange gloves on his hands.

To his right was the man Diego guessed to be former police chief, Brutus Howard. He matched Doug Trainer in his shiny black boots and jeans, but lacked the harness. On his head, he wore a black Doberman hood and there was no mistaking that the glittering metal on his fists were brass knuckles.

"Mierda." Diego pulled Alex into an aisle and crouched down. "I've got to find a place where I can change. I want you to head to the back and make sure everyone's okay, then head straight back home."

Alex kissed Diego. "Be careful, and remember, those gun blasts can disrupt your suit."

"You be careful." Diego hugged Alex tightly. "If anything happens to you, I don't know what I'll do. Now go."

Alex stood, then crouched back down. "If anything bad happens, I want you to know I love you."

"I love you, too." Diego pulled Alex into a kiss. "Now go, so we can save the day."

Alex stood and fought the crowd to get toward the stage. Diego watched him until he made it through the crowd and disappeared backstage. *Now to find a place to change.* Diego scanned the room. *Perfect.* Diego stood and pushed his way to a door on the opposite side of where Alex had gone.

He slammed his shoulder into the locked door. After two hard hits, the door popped open. Diego slipped unnoticed into the tiny janitor's closet. He flipped the light on, then pressed his left cufflink. His sports jacket and slacks began moving and changing colors. Shadow Guardian stood where Diego once did.

"Aaron, we need to get you and Felipe out of here." Juan Carlos pulled at his lover, but he would not budge. "Aaron!"

Taking off his jacket and slinging it on a nearby chair, Aaron then took off his tie and started rolling up his sleeves. "You go. These people need me."

"Aaron, don't be a fool," Felipe chastised. "What are you going to do?"

Aaron kneeled down. Pulling up his pants leg, he unholstered the shock gun he had borrowed from Alex's lab. "Whatever I have to do to ensure these people's safety, and that includes muzzling some mutts."

"I love you, you fool." Juan Carlos kissed him. "Be careful, and remember, I love you."

Aaron winked at him. "I love you, too. Now get your son to safety."

"Juan Carlos!" Alex yelled, running toward them.

Juan Carlos's relief at seeing Alex was short-lived. A muscle Pup in a button-up shirt tackled him and the two started wrestling on the floor. Alex's shirt was torn open. Using the element of surprise and his superior strength, the Pup pinned Alex to the ground.

"Go!" Aaron barked at Juan Carlos and Felipe. "I'll help Alex!"

Fighting every instinct he had to help, Juan Carlos took his son's hand and pulled him to the fire exit. "Let's go! We'll just get in their way."

Aaron raised the gun and shot the muscle Pup with a blast. He shook and went rigid before falling off Alex. He heard growling coming from the darkness. Six more muscle Pups stepped into the light. Aaron checked the charge on his gun. He hoped he had enough juice to take out the Pups.

"Get off me!" Alex yelled. Aaron turned to see two other Pups had a struggling Alex and were pulling him back into the darkness. "You guys are going to regret this! You ruined Aiden's shirt!"

Aaron heard the footsteps of the attacking Pups. He turned and shot one, sending him shaking to the ground. He was about to take aim on the next Pup, but another Pup crashed into him, sending his shot wide and into one of the support beams. The other Pups joined the first, slamming Aaron's hand into the ground until he let go of the gun.

With two Pups pinning his arms and one holding his legs, the last Pup straddled Aaron and began punching him in the face. "Cowards!" Aaron spat out a wad of blood. His eye began swelling shut. "Wait until my fiancé sees what you did to me." Aaron began growing light-headed. "Juan Carlos is going to neuter you all."

Juan Carlos's heart broke seeing the chaos in the streets. People were running for safety. Pups were looting anything of value and destroying the rest. Keeping his son in the alley, Juan Carlos said, "I have to get back to DJC Tower. Do you have any sort of command center set up?"

"Of course not." Felipe watched the anarchy in the streets. "I'm not the mayor yet."

Taking hold of Felipe's shoulders, Juan Carlos said, "This city needs leadership and you're it." Juan Carlos thought for a moment. "You can use the remote system in the apartment to coordinate the DJC City Guard. While I do what I have to do."

"What do you have to do?" Felipe asked.

Juan Carlos straightened his shoulders. "Protect our family." Juan Carlos tapped the tiny earpiece. "Can anyone hear me?"

"Um, hi," a hesitant Chitter came back.

Shadow Guardian came on the line. "Chitter, what are you doing on the coms?"

"Translating for Alegro while he helps Fire, Ice, and Sentry rescue Gaymer from some dude that calls himself Demon Twink," Chitter answered.

Confusion spread across Juan Carlos's face. "I thought Esmerelda banished him."

"Esmerelda banished someone?" Filipe asked.

Juan Carlos held up his hand to his son. "Not now."

"They've got Alex and Aaron," Shadow Guardian announced. "They beat Aaron up pretty bad."

Juan Carlos's nostrils flared. He grabbed Felipe's hand. "It's time to take these Pups to obedience school. Come on."

"What is going on out there?" Demona asked Herc.

Pulling the door shut and locking it, Herc answered, "It looks like those Pups that robbed the city earlier are rioting in the streets." He turned to Demona. "They are shooting at everything, snatching young men and women, then tossing them tied up into the back of a moving van."

"We need to go out there and stop them." Dion tried to get to the door, but Demona stopped her. "What are you doing? They need our help."

Demona let out a sigh. "We cannot. We are the caretakers of In Between so we are not allowed to interfere with the human or mystical worlds. We must remain neutral or suffer a horrible consequence."

"Juan Carlos, Aaron, Alex, and Diego are out there!" Dion pleaded. "They need our help!"

Taking Dion in her arms, Demona said, "I wish we could. We can't even ask for help on their behalf."

"You can't." Ryuu came up, with an arm around a tall, slender, tanned man with silky, white, straight hair falling down around his shoulders. "Andrea can."

Dion pulled away Demona. "Will you do it, Andrea?"

"Of course." Andrea's voice was soft yet majestic. "The only problem is, where do I get the help from?"

Demona raised her left hand. A small pinprick of light grew in front of her to the size of a person. "I know just the place."

Stepping out of the broom closet. Shadow Guardian scanned the room. Most of the audience was gone, escaping through fire exits and side doors, but the Pups were singling young people out, dragging them to Doug Trainer. Shadow Guardian watched Trainer raise his hand at the struggling hostages, causing them to go docile. A Pup hood was put on them, then they willingly joined the pack in destroying the city.

He's making more Pups. Shadow Guardian began making his way through the auditorium. A Pup came charging at him. Shadow Guardian punched him in the nose, sending the Pup staggering back. *At least it didn't squeak.* The Pup glared at Shadow Guardian.

"I've battled bigger dogs than you." Shadow Guardian extended his left hand, shooting a Shadow Dart into the Pup. His eyes glazed over. He staggered before falling down. Shadow

Guardian nudged the passed-out Pup. "Guess I'll let this sleeping dog lie."

Shadow Guardian moved along the edge of the stage to the center aisle. A massive muscle Pup blocked his path. "How many of you are there?" A Pup sneaked up behind him on the stage and jumped, landing on Shadow Guardian, and sending them tumbling onto the ground. "Bad boy!"

Shadow Guardian maneuvered his way from under the first Pup, only to be tackled by the second Pup and slammed into the side of the stage. Interlacing his fingers, Shadow Guardian brought his hands down onto the Pup's back. He collapsed onto the ground, but before he could recover, the first Pup's fist connected with his jaw.

Shadow Guardian jumped up to land on the fallen Pup's back. "You boys need obedience training." With one arm aimed down and the other at the advancing Pup, he shot Shadow Darts into them. *I'm going to run out of darts.*

"Can anyone hear me?" Juan Carlos's voice came over the coms.

Before Shadow Guardian could answer, Chitter hesitantly answered, "Um, hi."

"Chitter, what are you doing on the coms?" Shadow Guardian asked, shooting a dart at another advancing Pup.

Chitter answered, "Translating for Alegro while he helps Fire, Ice, and Sentry rescue Gaymer from some dude that calls himself Demon Twink."

"I thought Esmerelda banished him," Juan Carlos commented.

Shadow Guardian watched Pups dragging Alex and Aaron from behind the stage. "They've got Alex and Aaron." Shadow Guardian sent out a tendril to try to snatch Alex from their grasp, but another Pup jumped in the way. The tendril wrapped around him. Shadow Guardian pulled the Pup toward him. "They beat Aaron up pretty bad."

He punched the Pup in the nose, causing a squeak. *I don't know if that's cute or annoying.* Withdrawing the tendril, Shadow Guardian grabbed the Pup by the shoulder and sent an electrical jolt that sent him convulsing onto the ground. He scanned the auditorium for Alex and Aaron. He found them being forced to their knees before Trainer.

"Go!" Pup Brutus ordered the newly programmed Pup, "Destroy! Cause havoc!"

Trainer scratched the back of Pup Brutus's head. "Good boy."

"Woof," Pup Brutus said happily. "It looks like they have two more." He pounded his fist into his hand. "It looks like they've tenderized Aaron Heath for me."

Trainer put a hand out to block Pup Brutus. "Stand down. Having him running around destroying the city will ruin the trust the city has in him."

"Grrrr," Pup Brutus snarled. "Fine, but he's mine after."

Alex and Aaron were thrown to the ground in front of Trainer. "Look what we have here." Trainer held up a hand at them. "New recruits." Trainer scowled at their defiant smirks. "Why isn't this working?"

"It's not going to work." Aaron spat blood at Trainer's feet. "We found a way to neutralize your mind control."

Pounding his fist into his hand again, Pup Brutus snarled. "Does that mean Aaron is mine?"

"Bring them with us," Trainer ordered. He narrowed his eyes at Shadow Guardian advancing at them. "Pup Brutus, go turn that meddler into a chew toy."

Pup Brutus flexed his hands. "Gladly."

Pup Brutus stepped forward, past Alex and Aaron. Shadow Guardian stopped, waiting to see what Pup Brutus was going to do. Pup Brutus strode forward, clenching his hands tight. Shadow Guardian raised a hand, shooting out a dart. Pup Brutus dodged it. One of the Pups behind him made a whimpering sound, then fell over.

"Let's see how you like being on a leash." Raising both hands, Shadow Guardian sent tendrils out that Pup Brutus caught. They snaked through Pup Brutus's grasp and wrapped themselves around Pup Brutus's wrist.

Pup Brutus pulled the tendrils toward him, Shadow Guardian pulled back. "This Pup doesn't get leashed."

"Shocking." Shadow Guardian sent pulses of electricity through his tendrils, but before it could reach Pup Brutus, a blast from a Pup's shock gun sliced through the tendril. Microbots fell to the floor. "Hija de puta."

The tendril unraveled from Pup Brutus's fists and slithered back to Shadow Guardian, scooping up all the damaged microbots it could along the way. It reabsorbed itself and the damaged microbots back into the suit.

Pup Brutus growled merrily, "You have a weakness." Pup Brutus snapped his fingers. "Pup Patrol!" Four Pups rushed forward. "First one to hit him gets a chew toy."

The four men took aim and began firing. Shadow Guardian dove into the seats, narrowly missing the barrage. On his hands and knees, he crawled across the floor to the other end of the row. He stuck his head out the other side, but yanked it back when he saw a Pup about to fire at him.

"You're the Pup Patrol!" Pup Brutus bellowed angrily. "You should have better aim than that!"

Rolling onto his back, Shadow Guardian extended his arm to shoot a Shadow Dart toward the other side. A Pup appeared. He didn't have a chance to raise his weapon before the dart lodged into his arm and sent him falling to the ground. The Pup that shot at his head appeared above him. Shadow Guardian slammed his fist into the Pup's groin. Dropping his weapon, the Pup doubled over in pain and fell over, howling.

"At least that didn't squeak." Shadow Guardian jumped to his feet. He saw the two remaining Pups had flanked him, one several rows down, the other several rows up. They fired. Shadow Guardian dropped to the ground, letting the Pups take each other out.

"Shadow Guardian! Look out!" Alex shouted.

Shadow Guardian stood. He spotted the danger too late. Pup Brutus was charging him and threw a left uppercut with his brass knuckles. Shadow Guardian's head flew back. Warning lights mixed with stars in his vision. Before he could recover, there was another punch in his gut, then a series of cross punches into his jaw.

Two tendrils shot up from the dazed Shadow Guardian's shoulders. Attaching to the ceiling, they yanked him up, leaving a mad, howling Pup Brutus down below. He checked the suit's integrity. It was down to fifty percent, but was slowly climbing up.

Chitter buzzed in his ear. "Hang in there. Help is on the way."

"Poor choice of words." Shadow Guardian groaned.

Down below, Pup Brutus shouted, "Someone get me a big stick so I can whack this piñata!"

"Pup Brutus! Leave him!" Trainer ordered. "We have an entire city to bring to its knees!"

CHAPTER 30

UNDER THE LIGHT OF THE FULL moon, anarchy ruled the streets. The precocious Pups were leaving a path of destruction in their wake. Throughout the city, the terrified screams of the people could be heard. The streets were littered with shattered storefronts and destroyed vehicles set ablaze.

Stepping out of the auditorium, Trainer took a moment to enjoy the pandemonium. "I helped build this city into what it is. Now, I will watch it burn."

"What do you want me to do with these two?" Pup Brutus yanked Alex forward while another Pup pushed Aaron along.

Trainer sneered at his prisoners. "Bring them along. They can watch what happens when someone crosses us."

"You're a monster!" Alex tried to yank himself away from Pup Brutus's grip. "Shadow Guardian will stop you!"

Trainer laughed sadistically. "You mean that pathetic hero we left dangling from the ceiling?"

"Don't count him out yet," Aaron said, clutching his side in pain.

Trainer sneered in Aaron's face. "Let him try and stop me." Turning away, Trainer pulled out a whistle from his pocket. He blew it, sending a high-pitched screech echoing in the city. "To me, my Pups!"

Pups began appearing, heading toward Trainer and Pup Brutus. Some wore torn clothing, others had bruises and cuts that they ignored. Quite a few were recently converted and wore their masks awkwardly. A group of Pups were herding captured young people by gunpoint toward Trainer.

"New recruits." Trainer raised his hand. His glove activated, sending the powerful suggestion to Pup and prisoner alike to obey him. "Who needs to be mayor when you can be the alpha of the city?"

Pup Brutus addressed the pack. "Tonight we show the city who really runs it!" The Pups began barking their cheers. "Make your Trainer proud, Pups!" Pups began howling. Pup Brutus nodded to Trainer.

"You are all good Pups!" Trainer stepped forward. "Bring me the members of the city council and that foolish boy, Felipe Montoya! I want them kneeling at my feet!" A snowball hit Trainer in the face. Fuming, he wiped the melting ice away.

Pup Brutus stepped forward. He snarled, "Who dares challenge the Trainer?!"

"I do!" Moving her hover disc into the light, Ice threw a snowball into Pup Brutus's face.

Pup Brutus growled, "The Ice Queen."

"Just Ice," she corrected, pretending to examine her nails. "Don't get me wrong, I am a queen, but I just go by Ice."

Two small flying discs zoomed past Ice to knock the Pups off Aaron and Alex. "Hey, don't forget about me." Catching the returning discs, Sentry appeared by Ice. "You can call me Sentry."

"More foolish heroes." Trainer stepped forward. He raised his left hand to send the subliminal command. "Why isn't this working?!"

Ice pretended to yawn. "Are you having an ID 10 T error?"

"Alex, are you there?" Chitter asked through his com.

Pretending to scratch his ear, Alex whispered, "Yeah."

"Look up," Chitter responded.

Alex looked around, then up. He saw the third hover disc. "I see it. Can you get it to us without the Pups noticing?"

"Pups!" Pup Brutus shouted. "Bring them to your Alpha!"

Chitter chirped, "I hope so. If not, Fire is ready to provide cover."

"Aaron, are you up for it?" Alex asked, putting an arm around him.

Aaron looked up, then at the massive pack of Pups before them. "I don't have a choice, do I?"

"You guys really have bad aim." Ice hurled a barrage of snowballs into the Pups as she dodged the blasts of their shock guns.

Sentry took aim at Pup Brutus and hurled one of his discs. "Want to play Frisbee, Pup?"

"Arrogant punk!" Pup Brutus dove to the ground. Following the disc with his eyes, he saw Alex and Aaron rising up on one of the hover discs. He jumped up and charged them. "Where do you two think you're going?"

Several fireballs landed in front of Pup Brutus, stopping him in his tracks. Alex waved at him with his free hand. "Bye, Fido!" A shot from a shock gun hit the hover disc, causing it to malfunction. "Me and my big mouth!" Alex held onto Aaron as they veered off over the gathered Pups.

"Bring them down!" Trainer shouted.

Ice dodged a blast and zoomed up. "I'll grab Fire. You grab Aaron and Alex!"

"Easier said than done." Sentry caught one of his returning discs. A shock gun blast hit him from underneath. His hover disc began a downward spiral. "I'm going down!"

Chitter chirped into his ear, "Help is on the way."

"It better be quick!" Sentry braced himself for the crash. A black tendril wrapped around him and pulled him from the falling hover disc up onto the roof of the auditorium.

Shooting two more tendrils out to grab Alex and Aaron, Shadow Guardian said, "Nice moves out there." Their hover disc plummeted down, evading the rescue attempt. "Damn."

"A little help here!" Alex yelled, holding onto Aaron tightly.

Alarmed, Aaron shouted, "We're going to crash!"

"I got you!" Ice sent down a flurry of snow, creating a small snow bank for them to crash into.

Pups began swarming Alex and Aaron, pulling them from the snow. On the rooftop, Shadow Guardian ran toward Sentry. Stepping into his hands, Shadow Guardian was propelled up into the air. Doing a somersault, he began shooting

Shadow Darts at the Pups trying to retake Aaron and Alex.

Fireballs shot down past Shadow Guardian, clearing the area for him to land. An icicle shot up from the ground. Shadow Guardian gripped the slender ice pillar and began spinning around it until he reached the ground. Fireballs and snowballs rained down around him, keeping the malicious Pups at bay.

"Finish them!" Trainer roared from the side.

Ice hit Trainer with a snowball. "That's for Gaymer!"

"You're going to pay for that!" Pup Brutus snatched the shock gun from a nearby Pup and shot the Ice's and Fire's hover disc.

"Jump!" Fire leaped off the hover disc. Flames shot out from her hands, lowering her slowly to the ground.

Ice jumped, landing on an ice slide that carried her down beside her sister. "Are you okay?"

"Yeah, but remember that thing about being a superhero?" Fire held her flaming hands up to ward away the Pups. "I don't think I want to do that anymore."

Ice sent icicle darts into the guns of several Pups. "It's too late now." She created another ice slide. "Here comes Sentry!"

"Chitter says Juan Carlos is on the way with reinforcements." Sentry began punching and kicking the attacking Pups. "We need to get to the others."

Fire extinguished her hands. "I'm on it."

"Fire! No!" Ice reached out to her sister, but it was too late.

Above them, the whirling blades of several news helicopters could be heard. Fire ignited her entire body. Pups moved back from the intense heat and light. She moved forward, causing the Pups to part and allowing the trio to reach their comrades. With them back together, she doused her flame.

Turning around, she smiled weakly at Sentry and Ice. "I did it." The shot from a shock gun sent her convulsing and falling to the ground.

"Fire!" Sentry caught her. Kneeling down, he held her protectively.

Ice held up her hands by her side. "No one hurts my sister." A blizzard began swirling around her.

"Ice stop!" Alex yelled. "You'll freeze us all."

Shadow Guardian tapped his temple. "Chitter, where are those reinforcements?"

"Close," Chitter answered. "I think. I don't know how to work these systems yet."

The Pups parted for Trainer and Pup Brutus to approach. "Surrender or else," Pup Brutus ordered.

"I'm tired of you." Ice raised her hand to blast Pup Brutus, but he was quicker and shot her with a shock gun.

Shadow Guardian moved to catch her. "We'll never surrender."

"So be it." Trainer smiled. "Pups—"

The sounds of clacking horse's hooves cut Trainer off. Juan Carlos shouted from the darkness, "Trainer, you pissed off the wrong Drag Queen!"

CHAPTER 31

"I'M GLAD YOU LIVE CLOSE TO THE auditorium," Felipe said as he and Juan Carlos rushed into the penthouse. "But what am I going to be able to do from up here?"

Juan Carlos pulled him along into the living room. "For emergencies, Diego had a workstation installed." Juan Carlos tapped on a keypad on the wall by the television. The area under the television slid open and a chair and desk with various controls came out. "You'll be able to direct the DJC City Guard from here."

"What do I do?" Felipe asked nervously, sitting down in the chair.

Juan Carlos handed him a headset, then typed on the keyboard. The screens came to life with images of the chaos. "You're going to remember that you're my son, step up, and take charge."

"At least I'll have you here to help me." Felipe slipped on the headset.

Putting a hand on Felipe's shoulder, Juan Carlos said, "I wish I could, but I need to help the rest of our family."

"How?" Felipe looked up at his father.

Pulling out his phone, Juan Carlos tapped in the code. The floor opened, revealing the stairs leading down to Shadow Command. "We'll talk about it after all this mess is over."

"How many secrets are there in this apartment?" Felipe asked, a slight tinge of panic in his voice.

Taking a step onto the stairs, Juan Carlos said, "More than I can tell you about right now. You focus on saving the city. I'm going to save our family."

"Is there anyone in Shadow Command that can hear me?" Esmerelda's voice came over the speaker.

Chitter looked at Alegro, then asked, "Who is this?"

"Who are you and what are you doing in Shadow Command?" Esmerelda questioned.

Chitter's metallic hair bristled. "Rude. We asked you first."

"I'm sorry, I should know better," Esmerelda conceded. "This is Esmerelda, the Gitana. I'm trying to get a hold of Juan Carlos, but the calls aren't going through."

Chitter scanned the screen. "Cell and radio service is spotty due to the Pup panic. Towers are being overloaded."

"Who am I talking to and why are you in Shadow Command?" Esmerelda pressed.

Chitter waited for Alegro's signal before answering. "I'm Chitter. I'm translating for Alegro, who is running Shadow Command."

"The binary, non-binary life forms," Esmerelda said with a smile in her voice. "Are you able to get a hold of Juan Carlos?"

"No need. I'm right here." Juan Carlos stepped up to the console. He patted Alegro and patted Chitter on the head.

There was relief in Esmerelda's voice when she spoke. "I got Dion's message. Help is on the way." A mystical portal opened up behind the trio. "I can't get this one back to where he belongs, but I'm sure you can help him get home. Good luck, my friend."

"Andrea!" Juan Carlos rushed to hug the white-haired man that stepped through the portal.

Andrea hugged Juan Carlos back. "It's good to see you again, my friend."

"Where are the reinforcements?" Juan Carlos asked when the portal closed.

Andrea smiled. "They are on their way. We just need to join them."

"I'm no hero. My place is here in command," Juan Carlos argued.

Andrea pressed a finger to Juan Carlos's forehead. "You are a hero to many and your place is out front leading." Magic swirled around Juan Carlos. "You are Dolores Salvaje." Juan Carlos was transformed into his Drag persona, Dolores Salvaje. She stood there wearing a glittery blue bodysuit, flawless makeup, and impeccable high hair that cascaded down in ringlets. "Let's show these Pups who really rules this city."

"Alegro wants to go, too," Chitter chimed in. "He wants to help his daddies."

Andrea's smile sparkled. "The more the merrier. What about you adorable one? Are you coming along?"

"No, I've had my fill of Pups," Chitter barked. "I'll stay here and keep communications open."

Alegro zipped over to wrap around Dolores Salvaje. "How are we going to get there? The streets are filled with rioting Pups."

"In style." Andrea's eyes sparkled.

CHAPTER 32

"SO BE IT! PUPS—" TRAINER shouted.

Transformed back into his unicorn form, Andrea stepped forward. The sound of his clopping hooves cut Trainer's words off. Dolores Salvaje rode on his back, with Alegro wrapped around her body. Andrea's golden horn sparkled in the moonlight and his white mane and coat glittered like starlight.

Dolores Salvaje shouted, "Trainer, you pissed off the wrong Drag Queen!"

"What do you think you can do with your glorified sparkle pony," Trainer spread his arms out wide, "against me and my Pups?"

Dolores Salvaje clacked her fan open. Fanning herself, she said, "You have your pack and I have mine."

288

A blond man in a black bodysuit decorated with white musical notes appeared from the shadows to stand beside Andrea. Then there was a howl. Lobo landed between Alex and Shadow Guardian, teeth bared at the Pups. From Dolores Salvaje's outstretched arm, Alegro shot out and zipped through the Pups' legs to wrap around Alex.

"Alegro, you shouldn't be here! It's dangerous!" Discarding the remnants of Alex's shirt, Alegro formed a long sleeve crop top over his daddy's body. Moving up the side of Alex's neck, Alegro pushed his hair up, then came together to create a domino mask. "What are you doing?"

Chitter chimed in Alex's ear. "They're protecting their daddy." They then added, "Also, they are boosting our com signal so we don't keep going in and out."

"The shock guns," Shadow Guardian said with worry in his voice.

Dolores Salvaje slapped her fan closed. "No one is hurting my grandbaby. Siren, if you would show these Pups what you can do?"

"Gladly." Siren's eyes blazed magenta. He let out a long B-flat.

Lobo gave a toothy grin. "You guys are going to love this."

Magenta wisps flowed along Siren's song. They danced around the Pups, finding every shock gun.

The guns popped and fizzled in the Pups' hands. They continued on, circling Trainer's gloved hands. The woven circuitry went haywire. The hypno began to smoke, then caught fire. He frantically tried to put the fire out with his other hand, only to cause the other glove to catch fire.

"Get these off!" Trainer screamed in pain, trying to get the flaming gloves off. They began melting into his skin. Trainer dropped to his knees, screaming, "My hands!"

A blast of ice hit Trainer's hands. A weak Ice lowered her hand. "You don't deserve it, but Gaymer would never forgive me if I didn't help you." With Shadow Guardian's help, she stood. "How could you give him to the Demon Twink?"

Rushing to his lover's side, Pup Brutus barked at Ice, "He didn't give Gaymer to the demon twink. We left guards there to protect him."

"I thought Esmerelda banished the demon twink?" Lobo growled in Shadow Guardian's ear.

Ice pulled away from Shadow Guardian to stand on her own. "Then why did the demon twink tell us you promised Gaymer to him?"

"He took Gaymer?" Tears of pain and sorrow streamed down Trainer's face.

Pup Brutus hugged him. "We'll get him back, but first we need to take care of these meddling losers."

"You're still too weak." Sentry kept Fire from standing.

"I can help." Fire raised a shaky hand, but it fell back down.

Alex guided Aaron over to the pair. "Aaron will take care of her."

"It will be an honor." Aaron let Alex help him down. Sentry passed her over carefully.

Sentry stood, ready to fight. "How are we going to get through this?"

"Together." Shadow Guardian flexed his hands. "I wish we had more help."

Pup Brutus stood and addressed the pack. "Pups! Avenge your Trainer!"

"Your wish is my command," Lobo growled merrily. He raised his head and let out an ear-piercing howl. "Aroooh!"

Lobo's howl was joined by another, then another, until a chorus of wolves could be heard. The howling stopped. Glowing yellow eyes began appearing in the darkness. A massive silvery blue wolf stepped forth out of the darkness, snarling. Other wolves joined him, growling and snapping. They surrounded the Pups.

"Siren, did I not say that I brought my pack?" Dolores Salvaje asked sarcastically.

Siren laughed, "You did."

A group of men pulled off their hoods and ran back into the auditorium. "Cowards!" Pup Brutus shouted after them. The remaining Pups looked around frantically between the wolves and the heroes they had corralled. Pup Brutus shouted at them, "I said avenge your Alpha!"

Pups charged the entrapped heroes. Ice pelted them with snowballs. Alegro raised Alex's arms and began sending out tendrils, slapping and pulling the Pups' feet out from under them. Shadow Guardian and Sentry stood back to back, punching and kicking the attackers. Lobo charged them, lifting and throwing Pups back into the fray.

The wolves charged into the fray, knocking over and pouncing on the Pups. They dragged subdued Pups before Siren, then took off to rejoin the battle. Siren began singing a soothing melody, sending green wisps over the Pups that sent them into a peaceful slumber.

Using the fight as a distraction, Pup Brutus lifted Trainer up and guided his broken lover back to the auditorium. Propping him against the door, Pup Brutus told his love, "Go, find Gaymer. I'll take charge here."

Shaking his head in defeat, Trainer held up his damaged hands. "How?"

"Dante gave me something in case we needed it." Pup Brutus pulled off his hood. He held up a small vial with bubbling red liquid.

Trainer cried out, "No, you can't trust anything he gave you."

"Do we have a choice?" Pup Brutus looked back at the thinning pack. He kissed Trainer. "I have to protect you, like you protected me."

Trainer knocked the vial from Pup Brutus's hand. The glass shattered on the ground. The liquid bubbled as it began eating away at the concrete. It fizzed, then there was a puff of smoke. "Not with anything from that fiend."

"I love you." He kissed Trainer. "I have to do this ... for us." Leaving his hood with Trainer, Pup Brutus raced back into the battle.

Trainer reached out with one of his damaged hands for his lover. "Pup Brutus!" he shouted. He watched Lobo tackle Pup Brutus. Trainer closed his eyes. "I failed my pack. I failed my family."

"Where's Trainer?" Lobo snarled in Pup Brutus's face.

Pup Brutus struggled under Lobo's weight. "Get off me, freak!"

"He's over here!" Ice shouted, strolling up to a slumping Trainer. She sneered down at him. "What do you have to say for yourself?"

Trainer looked up with wet eyes. "Please, don't hurt Pup Brutus. He only acted out of love for me."

"Do you even know what love is?" Ice shot back bitterly.

Trainer looked over at the struggling Pup Brutus, then back up into Ice's cold stare. "Yes." Trainer forced a smile. "I saw it in Gaymer's face when he told me about you."

"He," Ice faltered for a moment, "told you about me?"

"He did." Trainer nodded. "I'll give you whatever help you need to rescue him from the Demon Twink."

"I'll see that you get the best medical help." Ice lifted Trainer up to his feet. "It's time to face the music."

CHAPTER 33

"Thank you for coming to our aid." Diego rubbed Lobo's, the lunar wolf, head.

He smiled. "I told you, you are all pack now. Pack looks out for pack."

"Does that mean I'm pack, too?" Chitter jumped onto Lobo's back, then scurried up to sit on his head.

Lobo laughed with amusement. "Especially you, my little squirrel friend."

"Exactly how am I related to this thing?" Freddy asked, laughing at Alegro zipping around him.

Alex scolded him, "They are not a thing."

"You're Alegro's tio. They are your nibling." Everyone stared at Diego. "What? When you have a binary, non-binary child, you have to do your research."

Alex wrapped his arms around Diego and kissed him on the cheek. "You really surprise me sometimes."

"Well, I am looking forward to getting to know my new nibling," Salvador said, strolling in with a sullen Aspen. He kissed Freddy on the cheek. "Did you tell them yet?"

Freddy returned the kiss to his lover. "Not yet. Why don't you do it?"

"Okay." Smiling, Salvador turned to the curious faces. "Freddy and I are leaving Atlantis and coming back home."

Hugging Salvador, Alex exclaimed, "That's great news!"

"I've really missed you!" Diego pulled Freddy into a tight hug.

Lobo let out a howl of joy. "That means you two can come visit me in Lunaray when Diego and Alex do."

"That would be awesome!" Alex's excitement faded. Putting his hands on his hips, he scowled at Diego. "Wait, I don't remember being asked if I wanted to go to the moon."

Diego crossed his arms defiantly. "You said I could take you on a vacation." Diego poked Alex in the chest. "I am going on one, and you're going with me. Get over it, and save that anger for the make-up sex later."

"You're right. I did agree to go on a vacation." Alex hugged Diego. He growled seductively in Diego's ear. "Oh, there's so much anger."

Lobo shook his head. "On that note, I need to get going."

"Wait!" Aspen called out. "Can you use your mystical wolf abilities to find Gaymer for me?"

Lobo cocked his head at Freddy. "Mystical wolf abilities?"

"He's new." Freddy shrugged.

Chitter jumped off Lobo's head and into Aspen's arms. "No need. I can find him."

"What about the Omega Protocol?" Aspen asked.

Chitter leaped onto the console, followed by Alegro. "It was nullified the moment I saw Gaymer." Alegro began punching buttons. "Remember when the Shadow Drone dive-bombed the Demon Twink?"

"Yeah." Aspen raised an eyebrow. "You missed the Demon Twink."

Chitter chirped in laughter. "We weren't aiming for him. We just wanted him to think we were." The monitor came to life. A map appeared with a blinking red light. "We were aiming for Gaymer. We shot him with a tracking device."

"Chitter! I love you!" Aspen scooped up the squirrel and spun around. He reached out and stroked Alegro. "You too, Alegro!"

"Alex, Diego." Juan Carlos's voice came over the speakers in Shadow Command. "Could you two please come up here?"

Alex pouted. "Guess that makeup sex is going to have to wait."

Struggling to sit up in his bed, Aiden winced. "You don't have to babysit me."

"I remember saying something similar to that when I was in your place." Joshua set a steaming cup of tea on Aiden's nightstand. "Juan Carlos said this will help. Aaron said it tastes horrible, though."

Aiden scoffed. "You're not making a great argument for drinking it."

"Drink it while I lecture you." Joshua pulled up a chair to his bedside. "Aspen told me you're not supposed to do what you did tonight."

Aiden sank back into his bed. "He's scared I'll burn myself out. Literally."

"It was amazing, but please don't do it again." Joshua took Aiden's hand. "You and Aspen are the best friends I've ever had."

Aiden winked at him. "I'm better than Aspen, right?"

"Of course," Joshua laughed.

Aiden smiled. "Good. Now go get your nail stuff. I'll do your nails while I build up the courage to drink that tea."

Upstairs, Juan Carlos and a battered Aaron sat on one couch with Felipe alone on the other. "Please, sit. Aaron and I have something to share with you." Juan Carlos motioned to the empty seats beside Felipe.

"Is there something wrong?" Diego asked, sitting beside Felipe.

Juan Carlos took Aaron's hand in his. "No."

"They told me everything," Felipe blurted out in disbelief. "You being Shadow Guardian. Freddy being that wolf creature."

Aaron squeezed Juan Carlos's hand. "We haven't told you everything. There's still one secret left to share, and we wanted to tell the three of you together."

"What is it?" Alex asked, taking Diego's hand.

Juan Carlos kissed Aaron on the cheek. When he looked at the trio on the couch, his smile beamed brightly. "Aaron asked me to marry him, and I said yes."

"That's fantastic!" Diego jumped from his seat to hug Juan Carlos.

Alex carefully hugged the bruised Aaron. "Congratulations!"

"I am so happy for the both of you!" Felipe maneuvered in to hug his father and future stepfather. "This night has been full of fantastic surprises."

Diego tapped his finger on his chin. "Wait, does this mean Aaron is going to be my—"

"Diego, I swear if you finish that thought, Alex is going to be a single father," Juan Carlos warned.

"It's over!" Dion hugged Demona.

The lights in In Between flickered. Demona groaned, "It's not over yet."

Dion looked around. "What's happening?"

"You're about to meet my parents." Demona pulled away and brushed out the wrinkles in her outfit. Two points of lights appeared before them, one red and one white. They expanded to form the outlines of two women. "Hello, mothers." Demona kissed the blonde white woman dressed in tight leather, then the cocoa brown woman in a white body-hugging dress. "These are my mothers, Hedon," the blonde white woman in leather nodded, "and Purity." The cocoa-brown woman nodded. Demona put an arm around Dion. "Mothers, this is my girlfriend, Dion."

Dion nervously smiled. "Pleasure to meet you."

"Pleasure to meet you." Purity's voice was a melodic song.

Hedon's smile made Dion uneasy. "She looks ravishing."

"What do you want, Mothers?" Demona asked, not hiding her annoyance.

Sarcastically, Hedon put a hand over her heart and said, "What? Can't your mothers pay their only daughter a visit?"

"I haven't seen you in over three thousand years." Demona crossed her arms. "Spill it."

Purity put a hand on Hedon's shoulder. "We must be better about seeing our daughter."

"Maybe we should try for another child? Perhaps one that's a little more respectful." Hedon licked her lips at Purity.

Dion whispered to Demona, "Should I leave?"

"You're fine." Demona pulled Dion closer. "These two, on the other hand, that's a different story."

Purity sighed. "After recent events, your neutrality is being questioned."

"My neutrality? Explain." Demona moved Dion behind her. Her eyes flashed one red, one white. "Now."

Hedon held up a hand. "Don't banish the messengers. We were asked to come here."

"You opened a portal for Andrea to get to Esmerelda to ask for help for your friends." Purity shook her head. "That is not very neutral."

Demona stiffened. "I sent him to where he asked me to go. I am not responsible for his intentions or actions once he got there."

"He just happened to know where to go?" Hedon accused.

Dion stepped forward. "I told him we needed Esmerelda."

"I see." Purity eyed Dion. "We shall share that information with the others."

Hedon's eyes flashed red. "I like you, Dion. I look forward to getting to know you."

"We'll have... what do those humans do?" Purity thought for a moment. "Eat, that's it. We'll eat together soon."

Dion interlaced her fingers with Demona's. "I'd like that."

"Demona, make it happen," Hedon ordered. She reduced down to a red orb, then zipped away.

Purity stepped forward and touched her daughter's shoulder. "Please do." She reduced into a white orb and zipped away.

"I'm so sorry about that." Demona took Dion in her arms.

Dion smiled wryly. "I'm your girlfriend?"

CHAPTER 34

DIEGO SNUGGLED WITH ALEX ON the couch in his office. "It's nice to just relax for a change."

"I get it. I said we can go on vacation wherever you want to go." Alex sighed. "On Earth."

Diego smiled impishly. "Even if it's clothing optional?"

"You're trying to get more makeup sex aren't you?" Alex accused.

Diego's chest rumbled with laughter. "Maybe."

"We are such an odd couple." Alex began laughing.

Diego pulled him closer. "I love our oddness. When do you want to go on vacation?"

"As soon as possible, before something else happens," Alex answered. "With everyone singing Felipe's praises for taking charge of the DJC City

Guard last night, Salvador breaking the mind control of the Pups with his song, and Trainer and Brutus behind bars, there's no better time."

Diego settled back into the couch. "If something happens, our trio can handle it with Salvador and Freddy's help."

"Then let's go." Alex pulled himself away. Standing and stretching, he said, "It would be nice to spend a little quality time with you that doesn't involve some supervillain."

Diego pulled Alex back down onto the couch. "Where do you think you're going?"

"Back to work." Alex laughed.

Diego grinned. "I had Aiden book us for a two-hour meeting after lunch." Diego chuckled devilishly. "I also gave Aiden an extra-long lunch."

Aiden downed more of his water before stepping into Doctor Tyson's laboratory. No matter what he did, he couldn't get the taste of the nasty tea out of his mouth. Doctor Tyson's back was to the door, so he didn't see Aiden come in. Not wanting to startle the man, Aiden tapped on the door. Doctor Tyson's head turned around. He didn't smile when he saw Aiden.

"Is there something wrong?" Aiden closed the distance between them.

Doctor Tyson returned to work. "No."

"Then why won't you look at me?" Aiden put a hand on Doctor Tyson's shoulder.

Doctor Tyson shook the hand off. "I'm not an idiot."

"Of course you're not," Aiden said, concerned. "Who called you an idiot?"

Doctor Tyson looked at Aiden with hurt in his eyes. "You didn't call me an idiot. You just thought I was."

"I don't know where this is coming from." Aiden took a step back.

Doctor Tyson grabbed a tablet off the counter and pulled up a screenshot from one of the news agencies from the battle last night. He thrust it at Aiden. "Really? He's just a friend?"

"What are you talking about?" Aiden looked at the image of him as Fire being held by Sentry.

Doctor Tyson snatched the tablet back and enlarged the image, then thrust the tablet back at Aiden. "Don't deny that's not you being held by the man you had me make a suit for. I'd recognize your eyes anywhere."

Aiden wanted to feel hurt, but his heart pounded with excitement. He set the tablet aside. "You recognized me by my eyes."

"Yes." Doctor Tyson turned back to his work. Over his shoulder, he said, "You can go now."

Aiden spun Doctor Tyson around and kissed him. "You know how to make my heart soar."

"What's going on here?" Doctor Tyson asked.

Aiden put his arms around Doctor Tyson's neck. "Yes, that is me as Fire in the picture. The other guy is Sentry, and he really is just a friend. Nothing more. I'll introduce you to him."

"Oh, I'm sorry." Doctor Tyson tried to pull away, but Aiden wouldn't let him. "I shouldn't have assumed."

Aiden rubbed his nose against Doctor Tyson's. "Tyson, you really don't know what a wonderful man you are, do you?"

Aspen stared at the red blinking dot on the map displayed on his computer screen. *I'll find you Gaymer. I promise.*

EPILOGUE

KEAGAN JUMPED AT EVERY SUDDEN sound he heard. In the distance, he could hear the fearful screams of people in the Southside. It drove him to rush home to his lonely one-bedroom apartment. He didn't want to encounter one of the rioting Pups that was terrorizing the city. Now, they were in Southside, but that was but a few blocks from his place on the outskirts of the industrial district.

He was almost home when he saw a small kitten in the middle of the road. The lights of a speeding black SUV were racing toward it. Keagan ran into the street, scooping up the kitten and tossing it to the other side right as the SUV hit him and sent him flying up and over the roof of the speeding vehicle.

He landed hard on the pavement. He felt the snap of bones from his body landing awkwardly. Unspeakable pain shot through his body. He struggled to breathe. He tasted the acrid coppery taste of blood in his mouth. Opening his eyes, his vision was blurred. He could make out the taillights of the SUV continuing on as if it hadn't even noticed him like so many others during his life.

The kitten he rescued came up to him and let out a mournful meow. It licked his face. Keagan smiled at it before coughing up more blood. Other cats rushed to surround him. He recognized some as the strays he fed. Peace came over him. He closed his eyes. The cats began mewling in sorrow.

The clack of heels echoed in the empty streets. Madam Zelda, using her walking stick, strolled out of the darkness. She paused to look up at the zooming heroes flying overhead. She smiled proudly, then continued on to stand before the broken young man clinging to life. She leaned down and stroked the tiny kitten. It meowed at her, pleading.

"I understand." She righted herself. "I will honor your wishes."

Around them, the shadows coalesced into the forms of two genderless entities. They were identical aside from their clothing. One wore a suit that sparkled with stars. The other wore a matching dress. They looked down at Keagan's broken body while listening to the cats' pleading. They then turned their attention to Madam Zelda.

The one in the suit, Destiny, proclaimed, "No."

"Tsk tsk." Madam Zelda waggled a boney finger at them. "You and Fate know that I cannot deny them their request."

Fate looked about. "You walk a dangerous line, Ancient One." The cats hissed at the cosmic beings.

"I walk the path set before me," Madam Zelda countered, smacking her walking stick against the ground, causing it to glow. "A battle is coming and you two cannot fully see the path that ones like this one must travel."

Destiny spoke. "Nothing is hidden from us."

"Did you see this moment?" Madam Zelda smiled mischievously. "Now be quiet and allow me to do my work. These felines have claimed this one as their champion."

Madam Zelda held her walking stick over Keagan. Her eyes glowed white. Her black hair streaked with gray whipped about in the windless street. The gathered felines started circling Keagan. Fate and Destiny's eyes began flickering rapidly as the shroud that hid Keagan's true path lifted.

"It is done," Madam Zelda announced, leaning back on her walking stick. The cats began purring and brushing up against her. Cheerfully, she told them, "You are welcome."

"How is this possible?" Fate asked Destiny.

Confused, Destiny answered, "I don't know, but we must find out."

"Do that. Now go before he wakes." Madam Zelda crouched down to brush some stray hairs from Keagan's face. Fate and Destiny faded away into the night. Madam Zelda addressed the cats, "That's the problem with all-knowing beings. They always think they are right."

Keagan stirred. "He is your responsibility now, little one." Madam Zelda picked up the kitten and placed it on Keagan's chest. "Before I go, a simple request." She tapped the kitten on the head with a glowing finger, then Keagan's forehead. "Find this puss's boots."

Madam Zelda stood and started walking away. She pulled her shawl tight around her. She looked up into the sky. "A storm is coming." She continued on, disappearing into the infinite.

"What was that?" Dante asked when he saw the body fly over the SUV.

Lip-Sync stepped on the gas. "A poor unfortunate soul."

"Let me go!" Gaymer shouted from the back.

Dante raised his palm at Gaymer. "Sleep." Gaymer slumped over. Death Drop began laughing hysterically. "Do you want to be next?" Dante warned. Death Drop covered her mouth. "That's better."

"Can't you open a portal for us to go through?" Lip-Sync complained, speeding through the streets.

Dante closed his eyes. "Battling those elementals drained my reserves. I have to save what I have left to bring back my cloned thralls." Dante opened his eyes. "Of course, if you weren't playing with that pretty boy, I wouldn't be this drained."

"I wasn't playing." Lip-Sync turned onto the freeway heading out of town. "I was flirting."

Dante closed his eyes. "Need I remind you of your soul debt to me?"

"That soul debt doesn't mean I can't have a little fun on the side." Lip-Sync began morphing back into her true form, a young man with a scar across his face and a milky white eye. "I can't wait to tangle with him again."

Dante stiffened. "An unexpected development." He sneered. "Lunaray wolves." Dante opened his eyes. They glowed crimson. "Time to bring my thralls home."

"What about Trainer and Brutus?" Lip-Sync asked.

With his eyes still blazing, Dante answered, "They can fend for themselves. I got what I wanted from them."

A young man clad only in a tight pair of green briefs ran from the secret facility under attack. Chest heaving, and his hair dripping with sweat, he stopped at the top of a hill and looked back at the only place he knew as home. It was the place of his creation and torment. He slipped on the pair of stolen shiny boots and a pilfered lab jacket he had managed to snatch on his way out during the turmoil.

He saw something emerge from the facility. The young man turned and ran, knowing it was coming for him. *I'm not going back! I won't go back!*

RECIPE

IN THE BEGINNING OF SHADOW Guardian and the Boys that Went Woof, you have Shadow Guardian and Lobo racing back to Shadow Command to punish Alex for eating the last slice of flan. Most people have had flan in one shape or form, but I grew up with it. Oddly enough, I never got a taste for it until I was older. It was a texture thing for me. Now I love it and make it myself.

I'm about to expose a major secret that could get me into a lot of trouble. Please, whatever you do, don't let anyone know I let you in on this major secret. Also, don't share this secret with anyone. Are you ready? Okay, the secret is: flan is not that hard to make and it doesn't take a lot of time or effort to make. Just timing.

For generations, mothers have chased everyone out of the kitchen because they were making flan, but what they really wanted was some quiet time. I swear the only time my mother made flan was when she was tired of all of us kids and wanted some quiet time to drink her daily beer.

Now my mother made flan with a can of condensed milk and a cup of regular milk. The recipe I'm about to share with you is mine, because I'm lactose intolerant. Yes, I know I should be more tolerant, but when it comes to lactose, I cannot be. It does not like me. Our relationship turned sour many years ago. Fine, I'll give you both recipes.

Okay, now for the recipe.

Flan

What you'll need:

- ⅓ Cup of granulated sugar
- 4 eggs
- 2 cups of lactose-free whole milk
- Another ¼ cup of granulated sugar
- 1 teaspoon of vanilla
- A dash of salt.

- A silicone spatula
- Blender
- Pan mold of your choice for the flan.
- Bigger pan to put the pan mold into.
- A fancy-smancy serving plate.

For those who enjoy their lactose:
- Replace the 2 cups of lactose-free whole milk with one can of condensed milk and one cup of whole milk.

Optional

- Frying pan.

Directions:

First, you're going to preheat the oven to 325 degrees F. Then, put the mold pan on a burner over medium-high heat. Some people use a frying pan. I use the same mold my mother brought over from Spain in the 1970s. Oddly enough, most of my pots and pans are older than me.

You're going to add the ⅓ cup of granulated sugar to the pan and watch it. Carefully move the sugar around as it caramelizes by moving the pan. Once a good portion of the sugar has caramelized, you're going to reduce the heat until all the sugar is a golden brown. Once it is, turn off the heat and set it aside.

If you're using a frying pan to caramelize the sugar, this is when you would CAREFULLY pour the sugar into the pan. Caramelized sugar is hot and it sticks to your skin.

In a mixing bowl, you're going to beat 4 eggs together. You'll add the 2 cups of lactose-free milk. (The can of condensed milk and a cup of milk if you're my mother.) Add the ¼ cup of granulated sugar. (Leave this out if you use condensed milk.) Add a dash of salt, and finally the teaspoon of vanilla. You're going to blend until all the sugar is dissolved.

Next, you're going back to pan mold. Carefully move the caramelized sugar around so it coats the side of the pan. This is where I use the silicone spatula to bring it up farther on the sides. Then, add your egg mixture to the pan. Next, you're going to take your other pan and fill it with about an inch of water. Set that pan in the oven, then put your mold pan in the oven.

Bake it at 325 degrees F for about thirty minutes. Honestly, mine takes about forty-five minutes. You can check your flan the same way you check cakes. The center should be firm and the knife should come out clean. When you finally have a clean knife, you can take everything out of the oven, again CAREFULLY.

Set the flan mold on a wire rack to let it cool while you discard the hot water. After about thirty minutes to an hour, you're going to move the flan to your refrigerator and let it set overnight. It can taste a little eggy if you don't give the flavors time to mingle. The next day, you loosen the sides of the flan with a butter knife. Take your fancy-smancy serving plate. You're going to put it on top of the flan and flip it.

The flan should plop down as well as all that delicious caramelized sugar. Lift the mold pan up slowly and you'll see the caramelized sugar spread out to coat your flan and the plate. Now, cut and serve. Make sure you get lots of the delicious caramelized sugar on every slice. It pairs well with a nice cup of coffee.

I'm also going to share with you the trick of cleaning the pan mold. Some of that caramelized sugar will be stuck to the side. Instead of trying to scrub it all out, fill it with water, put it on the stove, and let the water boil. The sugar will dissolve in the water and it'll make for an easy cleanup.

Flan is a simple dish that looks as fancy as the plate you put it on. Refrigerate unused portions for a week. It doesn't last that long in my house. Really, the hardest part about making flan is pre-planning when you're going to make it. Well, cleaning the caramelized sugar out of the mold pan, too, but I told you how to do that easily. Enjoy and remember, don't tell anyone how simple it is to actually make flan.

BOOK CLUB QUESTIONS

1. Alex and Diego have been together a while, and though Alex practically lives with Diego, he is reluctant to move in. Why do you think that is?

2. Demona explained to Dion that some of the mystical creatures use magical charms to pass as human in order to survive. This is an homage to previous generations of LGBTQIA+ that had to hide or pass. Do people still do that now? Would you?

3. Aspen and Aiden are extreme in their personalities, yet they fall for men who are their total opposites and you see a change in them. Do the people we fall in love with change us or do they bring out a part of us that we have hidden?

4. Juan Carlos explains that people use things like being a Pup, a Drag Queen, or even a superhero to bring out an inner strength and power. Do you agree with this? Defend your answer.

5. Felipe finds out that Diego was never adopted by Juan Carlos. Is it not what you say but how you say it that matters?

6. One of the things that attracts Aiden to Doctor Tyson is that he didn't talk down or dumb down things for him based on his looks. Do we judge books by their covers? Has anyone done that to you?

7. Pup Brutus is jealous of the attention Mayor Doug Trainer pays Gaymer. How would you have handled it?

8. You see a change of heart in Trainer toward the end. Is it because of what he has done or what he stands to lose?

9. Gaymer created Chitter because he needed a friend and didn't want to be lonely. Have you ever "created" a friend so you wouldn't be lonely?

10. Even though Aspen has a family, he refers to the others as his family. In the LGBTQIA+ this is called found family. Do you have people who are not blood relatives that you consider family? Explain.

Author Bio

ROBERT (ROBBY) J. LEWIS IS A writer based out of Charleston, South Carolina. He has brought you not only the Shadow Guardian series but the Someone Series under Robert Lewis. He has written numerous steamy film scripts for Noir Male and Icon Male and more recently agreed to start writing for Luxxxe Studios. You can keep up with Robby Lewis's latest releases, news, and antics via his social media or at www.robert-j-lewis.com.

D. LAMBERT
Rydan
Celebrant
Northlander
Esparan
King
Traitor
His Last Name

DANIELLE ORSINO
Locked Out of Heaven
Thine Eyes of Mercy
From the Ashes
Kingdom Come
Fire, Ice, Acid, & Heart
A Fae is Done

J.M. PAQUETTE
Klauden's Ring
Solyn's Body
The Inbetween
Hannah's Heart
Call Me Forth
Invite Me In
Keep Me Close
Heart of Stone

JESSICA SALINA
Not My Time
To Be Normal

KAIT
DISNEY-LEUGERS
Antique Magic
Blood Magic

KYLE SORRELL
Munderworld
Potarium

LYRA R. SAENZ
Prelude
Falsetto in the Woods: Novella
Ragtime Swing
Sonata
Song of the Sea
The Devil's Trill
Bercuese
To Heal a Songbird
Ghost March
Nocturne

PAIGE LAVOIE
I'm in Love with Mothman
Dear Galaxy

ROBERT J. LEWIS
Shadow Guardian and the
Three Bears
Shadow Guardian and the
Big Bad Wolf

T.S. SIMONS
Project Hemisphere
The Space Between
Infinity
Circle of Protections
Sessrúmnir
The 45th Parallel

9 798823 203326